THE

EDGE

the Bayview High series

After Dinner Barf
Beating Up Daniel
The Big Split
Crossing the Line
Dangerous Rivals
Dear Liz
The Edge
Making the Grade
Muscle Bound
New Girl

BAYVIEW HIGH

THE EDGE

H.G. Sotzek

Vanwell Publishing Limited
St. Catharines, Ontario

Vanwell Publishing acknowledges the financial support of the
Government of Canada through the Book Publishing Industry
Development Program for our publishing activities.

Vanwell Publishing acknowledges the Government of Ontario
through the Ontario Media Development Corporation's Book
Initiative.

Vanwell Publishing Limited
P.O. Box 2131
1 Northrup Crescent
St. Catharines, ON
Canada L2R 7S2
sales@vanwell.com
1-800-661-6136

Produced and designed by Tea Leaf Press Inc.
www.tealeafpress.com

Printed in Canada

Library and Archives Canada Cataloguing in Publication

Sotzek, Hannelore
    The edge / H.G. Sotzek.

(Bayview High, ISSN 1702-0174)
ISBN 1-55068-133-8

    I. Title. II. Series.

PS8587.O85E34 2004   jC813'.6   C2004-904111-8

For Peter, Samuel, and the Babe.
Happy family.
xoxo…

chapter 1

tall, black boots

The black, hollow eyes seemed to stare back at him. The hooded form was terrifying. Ethan Munroe squinted at the evil face and quickly closed his eyes. After a moment he looked hard at the skeleton. With a flash of his hand, he drew a curved line. The arc of the grim reaper's blade crossed the page. He made a few more pencil strokes. Now, light seemed to glint off the steel.

"Excuse me," a voice said. Startled, Ethan glanced up. There was a pretty girl with long, brown hair pulled back in braids. She was cleaning the tables around him. "That's some picture," she said. "I would've never guessed you had a dark side." She smiled and brushed her braids behind her back. Then she turned to clear away more dishes from the other tables.

Ethan was speechless. He watched as the girl moved through the crowd and back to the coffee counter. He had seen Kat Matthews around the halls at Bayview High. They hadn't talked before, even though they were both in grade eleven. Kat was in a league of her own.

He watched her as she listened to the band play. Her eyes were closed, and her head nodded in time with the music. He looked over at the stage. The lead singer was excellent. Ethan thought his name was Arby or something. He couldn't remember for sure.

Ethan looked around the coffeehouse. The Edge was busy on Friday nights. He loved coming here. It had everything. Great live music. Amazing hot drinks. A ton of cool people. Most of the round metal tables were filled with customers. A line of people stood at the coffee counter near the back of the place. Many of them went to college. Ethan knew some of the others from Bayview.

Then Ethan caught his breath and froze. He saw Shelby and Damon come through the front door. They had been together a month now, but Ethan still couldn't get used to it. One of his best friends was dating *his* Shelby. Ethan had had a thing for her since grade nine. A wave of jealousy flooded over him. Then he took a deep breath as they came toward him through the maze of tables. Part of him wished he could just disappear. No such luck.

Forcing a smile, Ethan spoke. "Hey, guys. I didn't know you were going to be here tonight."

Damon sat down across from him. Shelby squeezed in on the bench beside Ethan. They were crowded in, and their legs were almost touching. Damon reached across the table and put his hand over Shelby's. Ethan looked away.

"We thought we'd just stop in to see who was playing tonight. You know, see who was here," Shelby said. She gave Ethan a warm smile, and he melted inside.

"So how was the movie?" Ethan asked, trying to ignore Damon's hand touching Shelby. Ethan was trying not to stare at her. Her silky, black hair just brushed her shoulders, curling up at the ends. Her thick, black lashes framed her chocolate brown eyes. Ethan adored Shelby Patel and was sure he always would. Sadly for Ethan, Shelby only had eyes for Damon.

Damon and Shelby were gazing at each other now. She didn't seem to have heard Ethan. He cleared his throat and spoke again. "So…?"

"Oh! Sorry, Ethan. The movie was great," Shelby said, "if you like car chases." She rolled her eyes at him.

"Oh, come on, Shelby. It was more than that. What about that wicked tidal wave scene?" Damon said.

"*Right*," she said with a giggle. "Hey! Damon and I are going to get something to eat. Do you want to join us?" she continued.

"No, um, I'm not really hungry," Ethan said.

"Are you sure?" Damon said. "We're going to Lee's."

"No thanks," said Ethan. He didn't like to pass up a trip to his favorite restaurant. But he didn't want to spend more time with them than he had to.

Damon looked doubtful. "Really?"

"Yeah. It's okay," Ethan said. "Really."

Damon looked around. "Has Carlos been here tonight?" he asked.

"No. He's been in training. The basketball tournament is next week. I bet that our star of the Bayview Sharks is pumping iron right now," said Ethan.

"No doubt," Damon said. "I guess we'll see you later." He and Shelby rose to leave. She gave Ethan a warm but sympathetic smile.

Don't pity me, he thought to himself. Ethan forced a smile on his face. "Call me tomorrow. Maybe we can hook up then," he said, trying to sound positive.

"Great!" Shelby said. "Oh, wait, we can't tomorrow. Damon and I have tickets to the Phat Dogg concert."

Damon groaned and pretended to be annoyed. "Right…Phat Dogg…I can't wait." Shelby gave him a playful nudge. Damon turned back to Ethan. "Maybe we can do something on Sunday."

"We're going out with my sister. Remember, Damon?" said Shelby.

"Oh yeah. What about next week?" Damon tried again.

"Sure. Whatever. Give me a call," Ethan said. *I won't hold my breath, though.*

"Great." Damon held out his fist to Ethan.

Ethan paused for a moment and then broke into a grin. He tapped his friend's knuckles with his own fist. "Excellent!"

Shelby pulled Damon toward the door. "See you later, Ethan." Damon waved over his shoulder as Shelby dragged him away.

Ethan watched them leave. With a sigh he turned back to his sketchbook. He flipped the page and instantly became lost in the picture. This one was of Shelby. He gently felt the ink-soaked edges of his sketchbook. While staring at her image, his pencil fell to the floor with a quiet clatter. When he bent down, he was face-to-face with a pair of tall, black boots. They were laced up almost to the knees. Kat Matthews was back.

"She's beautiful," Kat said.

"Who?" Ethan said, startled. He almost banged his head on the table as he sat back up.

Kat pointed to the sketch of Shelby. "Your girlfriend," she said.

Ethan flushed. "Oh, the drawing. Actually, Shelby and I, uh, we're just friends. She's going out with Damon Sanders."

"Friends, huh? I see. *Interesting*," Kat said with a smile. "Well, I'd be flattered if I had a *friend* like you. She doesn't know what she's giving up, I guess." She reached across the table for his empty cup and brushed past Ethan's hand. Ethan flushed again.

"Are you an artist?" Kat asked him.

"No. I just like to draw." He covered the page with his arm.

"You go to Bayview High, don't you? You're Evan Manley, right?" she asked.

"Yeah. I mean, yeah, I go to Bayview. But I'm Ethan Munroe."

"Ooops! Sorry. Let me start again. I'm Kat," she said with a warm smile.

"I know." Then Ethan wasn't sure what to say next. In fact, he wasn't really sure why Kat was still talking to him. All he knew was that she was cute. And her green eyes were amazing. Kat was one of the coolest girls he'd ever met.

Then Kat turned toward the music. Ethan followed her gaze. She seemed to be watching the singer. The guy was leaning toward some short-haired blonde near him. He seemed to like her a lot. For a moment, Kat stared at the singer and the blonde. Her green eyes narrowed slightly. Suddenly, she turned back to Ethan.

"Do you like carnivals, Ethan?" she asked.

"Excuse me?" he said.

Kat looked down at Ethan's open sketch-book. Shelby's picture still was looking up at them. Kat closed the book and pushed it gently back to Ethan. "You know...roller coasters. Ferris wheels. Cotton candy."

"Yesssss," he said slowly. He still wasn't sure what she was talking about.

"Good, because I've been dying to go to the spring carnival. So, I'll pick you up here at seven o'clock tomorrow night. Then I'll drive us over to the fairgrounds."

Ethan stared at her as she walked away. *Did Kat Matthews just ask me out?*

Kat looked back at him and winked.

Ethan couldn't help smiling to himself. *Cool.*

chapter 2

wild child

Lights spun by as Ethan was whipped upside down. The sound of screams deafened his ears. Then he realized some of the screams were his own. Their small car made its way to the top of another hill. It seemed to be stuck there for a long time. Then, with a gut-dropping *whoosh*, they went down the other side.

Air rushed by him. The force of the drop plastered him into his seat. He tilted his head to the right. Ethan expected to see Kat screaming, too. Instead, she was laughing. The roller coaster car looped upside down. It twisted and turned. At last, it came to a stop.

Kat's light brown hair was windblown. An easy smile crossed her face. "Ready to do it again?" she asked him.

"Later," Ethan said, laughing. "Let's wait until my stomach falls down from my throat."

Kat laughed, too. They walked down the aisle of games, near the midway. The carnival lights flashed a rainbow of colors. Music blared from the rides. It was a perfect May night—clear and slightly warm, with a few stars overhead.

"Are you hungry?" Ethan asked. He pointed to the food stand.

Kat nodded. "But I thought your stomach was in your throat," she teased.

"I can manage," Ethan said. "What would you like?" They looked up at a sign in front of one of the food booths. There were hot dogs, pretzels, popcorn, and cotton candy for sale.

"Um…a giant pretzel, please," Kat said. Ethan ordered it and some popcorn for himself.

They walked back down the game aisle. The carnival vendors tried to lure them toward each game they passed. "Hey, pretty lady," one said. "Try your luck over here."

Kat smiled and shook her head.

Refusing to give up, a guy with a bright yellow vest tried. "Hey, buddy! Win your girlfriend a prize. How about this pink elephant? Show her what a man you are!"

Kat and Ethan looked at each other and laughed at the same time.

"I was right," Kat said.

"Right about what?" Ethan said.

"You *do* have a fun side," she answered.

Ethan was puzzled. "Er…I'm not sure if that was a compliment."

"A compliment," she said, taking his hand. "So, tell me about yourself, Ethan Munroe."

"There's not much to tell. What do you want to know?"

"Well…tell me about your family," she said.

"Okay. If you really want to know. My parents are divorced. They've been apart ever since I was a kid. I live with my mom and her husband, Paul."

"Ah, a stepdad. Do you hate him or anything?" Kat asked.

"No, Paul's a good guy. Sometimes a bit *too* good. He tries too hard to be my friend. But my mom is really happy. He's good to her, too. So I guess I can't really complain," Ethan said.

"What about your dad? Is he married again?"

"Yeah. Dad and Sue got married a couple of years ago. I even have a half-brother. Dawson was born this winter, in February. He's cute and everything, but he's loud. And man does he stink! But it's not like I see him very much. They're pretty busy with him. And my dad travels a lot for work," Ethan said.

"I see. So what's Sue like? Is she an 'evil' stepmother?" Kat teased.

"No. In fact, she doesn't really seem to be into the whole stepparent thing. She's a lot younger than my dad." Ethan rolled his eyes. "So what about you?"

"What *about* me?" Kat replied.

"Is 'Kat' your real name? I mean, is it short for anything?"

"Katya. I'm named after my grandmother. She was Russian. But I've always thought it was old-fashioned. Besides, nobody calls me 'Katya.' *Nobody*." She gave him a warning glare.

"Katya? I really like that. Don't your parents call you 'Katya'?"

Kat groaned. "No. They call me 'Katie.'"

"Cute." Ethan laughed.

"*Whatever*," Kat said, and made a face.

"I mean it! 'Katie' is good, too," Ethan said.

"Sure. If you're in grade two. That's the problem, though. They like to think that I am." Kat looked like she felt a bit uncomfortable. She changed the subject. "Hey, so tell me about your sketches. You're really good."

Ethan was surprised. "Do you think so? It's just a hobby. You know, something to do."

"You should think of doing it as a job," Kat said seriously.

"Get out!" Ethan said, laughing.

"No, I mean it! In fact, I think we'd work well together," Kat said.

"What are you talking about?"

Kat gave him a proud smile. "I'm coming up with an idea for a video game. It's going to be medieval. You know, dragons, castles, knights…"

"Cool," Ethan said.

"Yeah. But it's not going to be any of that macho stuff. No knights rescuing maidens. My game is going to have a heroine. She's going to be the one kicking some butt."

"Wow! Are you designing the game on the computer, too?" he asked.

"No, I'm just working on a storyboard. I do that on the computer," she said.

Ethan shook his head. "What's that?"

"You know…a storyboard. It's like a step-by-step plan of what's going to happen in the game. What it looks like…where the characters can go…that sort of thing," Kat explained.

"Oh."

"Yeah. I've figured out how the characters should look, but the scenes are taking more work. It's got to look real, you know. Castles are more technical than I thought. There are a lot of details. I'm not as good at that stuff."

"It sounds like a great game," Ethan said.

"So do you want to work on it with me? I mean, the stuff you have in your sketchbook is amazing." Kat leaned closer to him. Ethan felt warm all over.

"That would be great! But, what do you want to do with it? The game, I mean."

"Oh! That's the best part. I know a guy who has a contact at this company. They make video games there. Ray says this guy owes him some favors. He'd show our ideas to his boss. If his boss likes it, they could turn it into a real game!"

"That would be amazing! Are you sure you want me to help?" Ethan asked.

"Of course I do," Kat said. She reached up and wrapped her arms around his neck.

Ethan pulled her close for the softest kiss he ever imagined. "Excellent," he said. This time, he wasn't talking about the project.

"Excellent," Kat said back. Then she murmured, "Besides, Ray owes me."

A tiny thought went through Ethan's mind. *Ray? Who the heck is Ray?*

chapter 3

pick up

"Oooof!" Ethan grunted as he hit the pavement. He had been about to knock the ball from Carlos' hands. But Carlos had turned quickly, knocking him down.

"You're going to pay for that one, Carlos my man," Ethan said. He rubbed the scrape on his leg. He wasn't great at sports like Carlos was, but Ethan was giving it his all today. He pulled himself up and dove in front of his best friend.

This time, Ethan knocked the basketball out of the path of the net. The ball went to the right. He snagged it and dribbled in the direction of the net. Carlos was closing in behind him. Ethan faked left, then moved right. He spun around and saw that Carlos had moved to the left. Ethan grinned. With a quick jump and an easy throw, he let the ball go. It swished into the net. "The champ!" Ethan called out, with his hands in the air.

"Yeah, yeah. I think this is the first time you've beat me this year," Carlos said, laughing. He wiped his brow with the back of his hand. "Total luck. What's your secret today? Did you take some extra vitamins this morning?" He ran his fingers through his thick, black hair. Sweat had made it stick up in places.

Ethan picked up the ball and tossed it from one hand to the other. "You wish! I'm all about skill, my friend." *And an amazing date*, he thought with a grin.

"That's a first," Carlos teased. He made a quick motion and knocked the ball out of Ethan's hand. "Nope. Just luck." Carlos did a layup, sinking the ball. He caught it again and made a hard chest pass back to Ethan. Ethan caught it with a *thud*.

Carlos went to grab his bottle of water. He called over his shoulder to Ethan, "I'm serious. Something's going on. I can tell. When I called your house yesterday, your stepdad said you were out with some girl. What gives?"

Ethan tried to play it cool and shrugged his shoulders. He couldn't hide the grin that was forming at the edge of his lips.

"Hey, man. Did you have a date last night? Was Paul right?" Carlos took a drink of water.

"I guess," Ethan said. His grin was wide now. The thought of his date with Kat last night still surprised him. He couldn't believe how much they'd connected. Kat Matthews hadn't ever said a word to him before. Today, he couldn't get the memory of her salty kiss out of his head. And he didn't want to.

Then Ethan noticed that Carlos had stopped talking and was staring at him. "What?" Ethan said. He obviously had not heard a word Carlos had said.

"WHO did you take out?" Carlos yelled. He took another sip of water.

"Kat Matthews," Ethan answered calmly.

Carlos sprayed out some of the water by accident. He cleared his throat and laughed. "Sure. If you don't want to tell me, that's one thing. But we've been friends for a long time. Don't lie to me now." He paused. It looked as though he were choosing his next words carefully. "I know this thing between Damon and Shelby threw you off. They're pretty solid these days." Then he grinned. "But you don't expect me to believe you took out Kat. I can't believe she went from Ray Brady to *you*. It's not like you're some star like myself," he said.

Ethan studied Carlos. Then he sank the ball in the net once more. "You're right. Sorry, man. Kat took *me* out."

Carlos looked Ethan in the eyes. He tried to stare him into a confession. When Ethan didn't break, Carlos' eyes widened. "You're telling the truth! You went out with Kat! Oh man. How did *that* happen?"

"We met at The Edge. She works there, you know. She saw some of my sketches, and we started to talk. She's creating a video game."

"I'm impressed," Carlos said.

"Yeah. Some guy named Ray can help her. He knows a guy at this company where they make video games." Ethan stopped. *Ray*, he thought. "Wait a minute. What did you say about Ray Brady?"

"Ray and Kat used to go out. I thought you knew that. How could you not know that?" Carlos said. He shook his head. "He's a musician. I think he even plays at The Edge. You must have seen him there."

Now it was all coming together. "Are you trying to tell me that 'Ray' is Ray Brady? How is that possible? Wait a minute. Ray Brady...R.B. ...*Arby?*" Then Ethan remembered Kat at The Edge on Friday. She had stared at the musician singing to the blond-haired girl.

"Duh," Carlos said. "I'd be careful if I were you. Ray has a bad reputation. So if Kat is still in touch with Ray, she could be bad news."

"What do you mean?" Ethan asked.

"He was busted for dealing drugs last year."

Ethan grew quiet. "*That guy* was Ray? You don't think Kat had something to do with it?"

Carlos shrugged. "I don't know. But Ray is supposed to be a big-time user. Or at least he was. Do you think Kat could've gone out with him and not known what was going on?"

"Maybe. But so what? Even if Ray was doing drugs when they were together, that doesn't mean Kat was, too."

"I don't know. Just be careful," Carlos said.

Ethan wasn't sure what to believe. "Thanks for the warning. But I'll be fine."

"If you say so," Carlos said and backed off. Then he tried to lighten the mood. "So, Kat Matthews, huh? That's great. If she's what you want, I hope it works out for you."

Up until a few days ago, Ethan could only think of being with Shelby. Now it all seemed different. Today it was all about Kat. Ethan grinned. "Me, too."

chapter 4

let it all hang out

It had been one week since Ethan first talked to Kat at The Edge. Now he met her in the hallways at school. He talked to her on the phone at night. It was like he was riding his own private roller coaster. He would go from happiness to disbelief. Kat Matthews liked him. And the excitement of it all made Ethan feel pretty good.

Now he was going to see Kat again. Ethan looked at himself in the bathroom mirror. His light blue eyes stared back at him. He spent close to three minutes brushing his teeth. Afterward, he checked for trapped bits of food. He took a swish of Paul's mouthwash. Cupping his hands over his mouth, Ethan checked his breath. *Minty fresh.* He messed up his dark, wavy hair and then smoothed it back into place. *Not bad.* Next, he looked for zits. *No gross bumps.* Most importantly, he raised each arm over his head and sniffed each pit. *Ah, sporty. I'm good to go.* With that, Ethan made his way downstairs.

He sifted through the keys hanging on the rack by the back door. He searched for the ones to his mother's minivan. *Great. A minivan on a date. Times like these, I really wish I had my own car.*

Ethan's mother rushed around the kitchen. She was busy packing her faded leather bag. "Are you going somewhere tonight, Ethan?" she said, as she heard the car keys jangle.

"Yeah. Can I borrow your van? I'm going to…uh…meet someone," Ethan said. He wasn't ready to tell her about Kat yet. His mother would ask him a hundred questions before he could go out the door.

"No. I'm sorry, honey. I'm on my way to my book club meeting. Can I drop you off?"

Ethan stopped in horror. Just the thought of his mother dropping him off in her minivan made him cringe.

"Mom, I really need to drive tonight. Maybe I could drop you off instead?"

"No, that won't work. I have a library board meeting later. You can always take the bus," she suggested. She started to say something else but then stopped and gave him a closer look. "Oh, you look nice! Do I smell cologne, too? Where did you say you were going?"

Ethan was about to answer when the back door opened and his stepfather came in. Paul crossed the kitchen and gave Ethan's mom a big, fat kiss. Ethan rolled his eyes.

When they pulled apart, Paul took one look at Ethan. "Hot date tonight?"

"Um…sort of," Ethan said.

Ethan's mother turned back to look at him again. "Really? A date? That's just wonderful! Who is it? Do we know her? Is it that lovely Shelby Patel?" Her face was beaming.

"No," Ethan said quickly. He was anxious to change the subject. He certainly didn't want to discuss Shelby with his mom. And he'd just started to date Kat. He wasn't ready to get the third degree about her, yet. "I guess I'll take the bus," he said and made his way to the door.

"I think it would be better if I dropped you off. It would be a good chance to meet your special friend," his mom said.

Ethan groaned. *I can't believe it. This keeps getting worse by the minute.*

Paul laughed. "Ethan can't meet a girl with his mother around! And he can't take the bus."

Ethan felt hopeful. *Please,* he prayed.

27

Paul just shook his head. "Here you go," he said, tossing his keys to Ethan. "Take my truck tonight. Have a good time."

Ethan felt relieved. "Thanks, Paul. You really saved me."

He was already out the door when he heard his mother call after him. "You didn't tell us who you were going to see!" Ethan pretended not to hear her as the door closed behind him.

Ethan always felt more like a man in Paul's black pickup truck. His mother's pale blue minivan wasn't cool by any means. But tonight when he drove to Kat's house, Ethan felt like *the man*. Then he pulled into her driveway and realized just where the heck he was.

When he got to Kat's front door, he realized he was sweating and nervous. Ethan was just about to ring the doorbell when the door opened. His finger was still in the air above the button. Startled, he jumped.

There was Kat. Her hair was loose today. It fell around her shoulders and brushed the edges of her face. "Hey," she said, with a lazy smile.

"Hi!" Ethan said. His mouth felt dry. They both just stood there, staring. Finally, Ethan spoke. "Uh…can I come in?"

"Oh…yeah…sure," she said. Kat slowly moved out of the doorway, letting Ethan into the house. "I'm hanging out downstairs." She led him through her house and into the basement.

It was amazing down there! It looked like something out of the seventies. There was a stereo with huge speakers. Old movie posters. A mirrored bar. A huge pool table.

"This is great! I love retro stuff," Ethan said.

"Yeah," Kat said. "Me, too." She slumped onto an orange beanbag chair. Kat leaned back in the soft, round mound and smiled at him. She began to nod her head in time with the music.

Ethan sat on the edge of a green leather sofa. He tried to relax, so he leaned back. Then he became aware of a strange sweet scent in the air. He had smelled it before at a concert at the beach last summer. *That couldn't be what I think it is. Or is it?* he wondered. He turned his head, looking for the source of the smell. Ethan started to get a bad feeling. Like something was wrong. *Maybe Carlos was right*, he thought.

"What are you looking for?" Kat asked.

"Oh. I smell something…uh…sweet."

She tipped her head in the direction of the bar. "Jasmine," she said.

Ethan looked at her curiously. *What the heck is jasmine?*

"I just love jasmine incense. I lit a stick earlier. Do you like it?" Kat continued slowly.

Ethan shrugged. He had never smelled jasmine before. He stretched to look, and he saw the smoldering, thin stick on top of the bar. A trail of smoke wound its way up from the slow-burning tip. A small pile of ashes had dropped off onto the bar. *Well, that explains the smell.*

"It was beginning to stink like wet dog down here," Kat said.

"Oh. I didn't know you had a dog," he said. At that moment an overweight, black, shaggy-haired dog lumbered past Ethan. It stopped to sniff his pant legs. Then it slowly pulled itself onto the couch beside him. The animal looked like it weighed one hundred pounds. A gray patch of fur ran down the middle of its back.

"That's Bongo," Kat said. "We've had him forever. Say hello to Ethan, Bongo." Kat giggled. "He's pretty relaxed."

So are you, Ethan thought.

They sat in silence for what felt like a long time. Ethan wasn't sure what to say next. Kat didn't seem like she was going to speak any time soon. Ethan cleared his throat. "I'm...uh... glad you asked me over today."

Kat smiled. "Me, too." The music seemed to cause her mind to wander. Then she turned back to Ethan, as if she had just noticed him. "Oh. Do you want something to drink?"

"Sure," he replied.

"Cool," she said and remained sitting.

Ethan paused. "Okay…uh…should I get it myself?" he asked.

"Okay," she said and then closed her eyes. She looked as if she was lost in the music. The sound of a slow guitar solo filled the room.

Ethan went to the bar and looked around. *Maybe there is a mini-fridge back here.* He found what he was looking for. Inside, it was packed with beer cans and bottles of wine. Way in the back he found a can of cream soda. "Do you want something, too?" he asked her. Kat shook her head slowly.

Ethan sat down again. Kat looked over at him. "You've got gorgeous eyes," she said. Then she got up, plopped herself on the sofa, and cuddled with him.

Ahhhh. This feels good, Ethan thought. *Maybe she'll look up and then we can—*

Just then the doorbell rang, and it wouldn't stop ringing. "Are you going to get the door?" he asked her finally.

"I guess," she said. Kat pulled herself off the couch and went upstairs.

Ethan leaned back and sighed loudly. He ran his hands through his hair. Then he stood up and walked around the room. *Who is she talking to?* Muffled voices floated down the stairs. He could make out bits and pieces of what was being said. From what he could figure out, Kat was talking to some guy.

"What are you doing here?" she said.

"Thought I'd stop by. You know, just hang out," said the guy.

"Well, I'm busy," she said.

"Doing what? Maybe I'll keep you company," he said.

"Not tonight," Kat answered.

"Oh yeah? Is someone here? Whose truck is in the driveway?" said the guy.

"Oh that. No one. Just a friend," Kat answered.

Just a friend? Ethan thought. *What's going on? What about our date? Does she kiss all her friends like that?*

Then the voices got muffled again. Ethan couldn't make out another word. He noticed the pool table and set up the balls. He grabbed a pool cue and hit the white pool ball with all his might. *CRACK!* The red ball knocked hard off the side bank and dropped into the far pocket.

Kat returned at last.

Ethan tried to act as if he had not heard a thing. "Who was at the door?" he asked calmly.

"Oh…um…just a friend," she answered.

"Anyone I know?" Ethan asked.

"I don't think so. Ray hangs out with people from Port Hope High."

"Ray Brady? Isn't he your ex-boyfriend?"

Kat shrugged her shoulders. "Yeah, we used to date. It didn't work out. Us as a couple, I mean. But we're still cool. You know…friends."

Ethan took a deep breath. "What does that mean? Do you still like him?"

She broke into a slow grin. "Hey, you don't think Ray and I…ah, Ethan, you're cute. No worries, babe. I've got someone else on my mind now." She moved forward to put her arms around his shoulders. Ethan felt confused. But Kat was holding him now. And it felt good. *Maybe I'm wrong*, he hoped.

Kat reached up and kissed him warmly.

Then Ethan just stopped thinking.

chapter 5

can you see me now?

Ethan slept late on Saturday morning. He woke up with a smile on his face. He was dreaming of Kat. Then he remembered what had happened the night before. He couldn't quite figure out what was going on. *What was Ray doing there? She said Ray was just a friend. But she told him I was just a friend, too. And what was up with Kat? She was acting really out of it.*

He went straight to the kitchen and looked for something to eat. Ethan found a note from his mother on the counter. She had taken three phone messages for him. The first was from Kat. Ethan's heart raced with excitement. He picked up the telephone and dialed her number. A man answered. His voice was gruff. Ethan thought it must be Kat's father.

"Uh, hello?" Ethan said nervously. "May I please speak to Kat?"

"Katie isn't home right now," her father said. "She's out with her boyfriend. Do you want to leave a message?"

BOYFRIEND?!!! But I'm right here! What is this guy talking about? Ethan thought. *Does he mean that she's out with Ray?* "Yeah. Just tell her that her *friend* Ethan called," he said angrily.

"Ethan? I didn't know Katie had a friend named Ethan."

"I didn't think so. Just tell her to call me when she figures things out. Thanks," said Ethan. Before Mr. Matthews could say another word, Ethan hung up. "I can't believe this!" he said to himself. He paced around the kitchen until he calmed down. Ethan read the other two phone messages.

The second one was from Carlos. He was going to need Ethan's geography notes next week. He would be away at the basketball tournament. The third was from Damon. He wanted Ethan to get some food with him and Shelby. "No thanks, guys," Ethan muttered to himself. He decided to call Carlos.

Carlos' mother answered the phone.

"Hello, Mrs. Diego. May I speak to Carlos?" Ethan said.

"Ethan, is that you?" she asked cheerfully.

"Yes, I have a message to call him."

"I'm sorry. Carlos just left for the tournament. He won't be home until Wednesday. Do you want to leave a message?"

"Just tell him I'll drop off the notes he needs on Wednesday night."

"Of course. It's good to hear from you, Ethan. Basketball season will be over soon. Maybe we'll see more of you around here," Mrs. Diego said.

"Sounds good," Ethan said. "Bye."

He spent some of the day doing homework. The rest of the time he was shooting hoops in his driveway. By dinner, he decided to see what they would be eating. Maybe they could order a pizza tonight. No one was in the kitchen, so he went upstairs. Ethan knocked on his mother's bedroom door.

"Come in!" said his mother.

"Hey, Mom. I thought we could order a pizza tonight," Ethan said as he pushed open the door.

His mother was standing in front of the full-length mirror. She had on a dark-blue evening dress. It was so long it brushed the carpet. She was putting in her special dangling earrings. They sparkled in the light.

"Wow! You look great! You didn't have to get dressed up for me," he joked.

Ethan's mother turned around and smiled back at him. "Thanks, honey. Paul and I are going out tonight. He's going to receive an award for advisor of the year!"

"Oh. So then you don't want pizza? I guess there'll just be more food for me," Ethan said with a grin.

Paul entered the room, carrying his black suit jacket. "Lisa, would you please tie this for me?" He pointed to the black tie hanging around his neck. "Hello, Ethan," he said and laid his jacket on the bed.

Ethan watched his mother work with Paul's tie. She laughed as she fumbled with it. "I think your neck has grown bigger since the last time you wore this, Paul."

"My neck didn't grow. The tie must've shrunk," he said.

"Of course it did," she said playfully. "Now keep still." When she finished, Paul gave her a huge kiss on the lips.

"You'll smudge my lipstick, Paul!" she said and gently swatted him away.

"Oh, you loved it!" he said, laughing. He turned his attention to Ethan. "So do you need money for pizza?" He pulled a few bills from his pocket. "This should be enough. Are you going to see your dad tonight, too?"

"I think so. Can I borrow your truck?"

Paul nodded. "Take your mother's set of keys. They're on her key chain."

Ethan looked at his stepfather and said, "Thanks, Paul. And that's great about that award thing."

Paul patted him on the back. Then he looked at his watch. "Come on, Lisa," he said. "We're going to be late!"

"Have a good time," said Ethan.

Ethan's mom gave him a quick kiss. Then she fixed her lipstick, smoothed a few loose pieces of hair, and adjusted her necklace. She and Paul happily brushed past Ethan and swept out of the house. In a moment, they were gone.

Ethan looked down at the money in his hand. *Maybe I'll order some food when I get over to Dad's*, he thought.

Twenty minutes later, Ethan knocked on his father's front door. He had a key and his own room there, but it didn't feel like home to Ethan. He felt more like a guest.

There was no answer, so he let himself in. Ethan heard sounds coming from the kitchen. Sue, his stepmother, looked up as he walked into the room. As always, she looked exhausted.

She had the portable phone squeezed between her shoulder and ear. Ethan's half-brother was on her other shoulder. The baby was howling. Sue was trying to warm a bottle with one hand.

"Hang on a second, Mom." She put the phone on the counter. She rocked back and forth to quiet the screaming, red-faced child.

"Hi, Sue. Rough day?" Ethan said.

Sue gave Ethan a tired look. "What do you think?" The baby kept crying.

Ethan took a quick glance around. There were dishes all over the counter. A pot of something was boiling over on the stove. Steam filled the air. "Let me help," he offered. He made a motion to take the baby. Sue hesitated when he came near. "It's okay," Ethan said. "I won't drop him or anything."

"Um…maybe you can take care of that pot," Sue suggested. She nodded toward the mess on the stove.

"Sure." Ethan grabbed a cloth and started to wipe it up. "Is my dad home?" Ethan hadn't seen his dad in three weeks. He'd been on a business trip the last time Ethan was supposed to stay over.

Sue made a face that let Ethan know he had touched on a nerve. "No. He's away on business. A sales meeting this time. And here I am up to my neck in dirty diapers. All alone. Again!" It looked like she was going to cry.

She picked up the phone again. "I'm sorry, Mom. What were you saying? Uh huh. No, we aren't planning on having any more children. How can you ask me that with Joe gone all the time? No! He absolutely said he only wants one child, too."

Ethan raised his eyebrows. *Just one? What about me?* He crossed his arms and stared at his stepmother in disbelief. He knew Sue wasn't excited about being his parent. But he couldn't believe his own father felt the same way. *You can't be serious. Is that why Dad doesn't spend time with me anymore? Because he has enough with his new son? I don't need this.*

"Well, since Dad isn't home, I think I'd better go now," Ethan said to Sue. "You seem to have your hands full, anyhow. See you later."

His stepmother nodded briefly and then went back to her phone call. Ethan pushed hard on the back door. It slammed behind him with a loud bang.

chapter 6

mr. nice guy

"**N**ow what?" Ethan said as he got back into the truck. He positively wasn't going to The Edge. At least, he was pretty sure he wasn't going to go there. He didn't know if Ray would be singing that night. Kat had said she and Ray were just friends, but Ethan didn't know what to believe. He just knew that he didn't want to be around the guy. *I mean, she was out with Ray this morning. And her dad still calls him her boyfriend,* he thought.

Ethan drove around the city. He found himself going down familiar streets. He ended up in a large parking lot. He looked up at the coffeehouse, sighed, and shook his head. Whether Ray was there or not, Ethan had nowhere else to go. He had nothing else to do.

"The Edge" was written across the black awning. There was a huge window in front. On it there was a picture of a large, tilted coffee cup. Three wisps of steam curled upward from it. An outdoor patio ran along one side of the building. Ethan grabbed his sketchbook and swung open the door to Paul's truck. He could hear music spilling into the parking lot.

Inside, Ethan made a quick scan around the room. Long brown braids. A wave of panic flooded him. Then, the girl turned around. *Not Kat*, he sighed. He made his way to his usual table near the patio window. It was the perfect spot for sketching. During the day, the window let in a lot of light. His seat was also in the perfect spot to see everyone who came in the door. He had a good view of the rest of the coffeehouse, too. Ethan dropped his jacket on the chair to save his seat. Then he went to the back counter to order a drink.

Kat's boss was working behind the counter. His nametag read "Troy."

"What will it be?" Troy asked.

Ethan looked up at the sign. A ton of drinks were listed on the board. There were whipped drinks. Steamed drinks. Drinks that seemed so strong they would melt your face off. "I'll have a super mug of hot chocolate, please."

After Ethan paid, he stood in a small lineup, waiting for his hot chocolate. He had a clear view of the drinks as they were being made. The coffee machine let out a threatening hiss and a great puff of steam. Finally, his own drink was ready. He carefully sipped it as he wound his way to his window seat. Ethan slid in and opened his sketchbook. *Ahhhhh. Now this feels like home.*

He looked around the room, searching for someone to sketch. Saturday night was a good night for checking out people. Date night. There was going to be some good music, too. He watched the musicians on the stage. A pretty woman with long, curly hair was singing. Her partner was great on the guitar.

Ethan spotted an older woman with frizzy, white hair. Her lipstick was deep red. Her eye shadow was bright blue. A long set of orange beads hung around her neck. *Now* she *looks like an interesting subject.* Ethan pulled out his pencil and began to draw. Soon he had a rough outline of her face.

"She was right. Your stuff is good," a voice behind him said.

Ethan whirled around in his seat. "Wha—"

A girl with a silver nose ring was grinning at him. Her black hair was pulled back in hundreds of tiny braids. They were piled on top of her head. Ethan read her nametag—"Tamika."

"Who are you talking about?" Ethan said.

"Kat, of course!" Tamika said. "She's not working tonight, you know."

"Oh. What makes you think I'm here to see Kat?" he said, trying to play it cool. The girl grinned and shrugged, but she didn't say anything. "I came here to sketch. And listen to the music. And people watch."

Tamika just looked at him. "Of course you did," she said with a wink. "You know," she continued, "I've known Kat for a long time. You're not her usual type."

Type? Am I a type? Ethan wondered. "Oh yeah? What type am I?" he asked.

"Nice," Tamika said.

What does she mean by that? Ethan thought. "Nice? What makes you think I'm 'nice'?"

Tamika gave a warm laugh. "Look at you. You're wearing a collared shirt. Your pants look like they've been ironed. And is that a picture of a minivan on your key chain? You couldn't be wild if you wanted to. Hey, it's not a bad thing. You just seem like a good guy. A guy you can trust. Depend on. You know…nice."

Ethan looked down at his clothes. He saw his mother's key chain lying on the table. There was a photo of the minivan lying in plain view. Ethan groaned and tried to hide it with his hand. "Okay. So what's wrong with being nice?"

Tamika set her tray on his table and sat down. "Nothing. Relax. It's a compliment! Look, I *know* Kat. I love her like a sister. But I've also seen her make some dumb choices. Like sometimes she doesn't have the best taste in guys. She's been burned before. I just don't want to see her get hurt again."

"Who is going to hurt her? Does Kat still like…someone else?" He didn't want to say Ray's name. Thinking about him was bad enough.

"I don't know," said Tamika. "I hope not. He really messed up her head the last time." Tamika met Ethan's gaze. She grew quiet. "Don't worry about it, Ethan. I don't know what she thinks about Ray. She doesn't talk much about him anymore. But I do know something. She really seems to like you."

"Did she tell you that?"

"She can tell you herself." Tamika stood up and looked past Ethan.

Ethan turned to see what Tamika was talking about. There stood Kat.

"Hi, Ethan," Kat said quietly. "I think we need to talk."

chapter 7

and nothing
but the truth

It was like time stood still. The singer's voice floated through The Edge. The words filled Ethan's head. "Just when I thought I had it all figured out. Then you came along…"

"Can we talk?" Kat repeated.

Ethan shrugged. "Sure. If you want, I mean." He pointed to the other chair at his table.

Tamika gave her friend a small hug. "I think I'll leave you two alone. Besides, Troy is giving me the evil eye. I'd better get back to work."

"So how are you doing?" Kat said to Ethan.

"Fine," he replied.

"Are you sure? My dad told me that you called," Kat asked.

"Yeah. I called. He told me where you were," he said. Ethan stared hard at her.

"Oh. I see." Kat looked him in the eyes. "You know, it's *really* over between us."

Surprised, Ethan's eyes grew wide. *But we barely even started!* he thought.

"Ray and I. We're really through."

He sighed. "Oh. Ray. Well, it didn't seem like that to me."

"What are you talking about?"

"Last week at your house. You guys sounded close. Like you were about to pick up where you left off. Then your dad told me you were with your *boyfriend* this morning. And I know you weren't with me. What am I supposed to think?"

"Forget what my dad said. He doesn't know anything. As for Ray, I know you don't have to believe me. But I want you to. It's hard to explain. Ray means—meant—a lot to me. But we're over now. Honest."

"Uh huh. So why was he at your place last week? Why were you with him this morning?"

"He just likes to hang out with me. Ray forgets that we're over," she said.

"Well, what did you mean when you told him you and I were *just friends?*"

"I didn't say that."

"Yes, you did. That night I was over. I heard you tell him, Kat," Ethan said.

"Oh. I didn't realize I said that," she said quietly. "Look, I'm sorry, Ethan. I didn't mean anything by it. I didn't mean to hurt your feelings or anything."

"That's good," he said.

"I'm sorry," Kat said again.

Ethan nodded. "Thanks," he said softly. "So, are we being honest here?"

She looked him in the eyes. "Yes. Why don't we start over? What do you want to know?"

"Well, there *was* something else about that night," he said.

Kat nodded. "Okay…"

"Did you smoke up before I got there?"

Kat blinked. "Wow. You were serious when you said you wanted to be honest."

Ethan nodded. "I've been thinking about it a lot. You were different."

"What do you mean?"

"You were *really* relaxed. More relaxed than usual. And there was that smell in the room…" Ethan trailed off.

"So what if I did?" Kat said calmly.

"Were you high?" he continued.

"Yes."

"Oh," Ethan said. "So…was that the first time you did it?"

"No," she said plainly.

"Really?" he blurted out.

Kat smiled. "Really. But it's not like I do it all the time, you know."

"Oh. So, when?"

"I don't know. Whenever I need to relax. I guess I was nervous about seeing you again."

"*You* were nervous?" he said. He couldn't believe Kat Matthews would ever get nervous.

"Sure," she said shyly. "I really wanted you to like me. I've never gone out with anyone like you before." A wisp of hair fell over her eyes. She gently brushed it back into place.

"Ah. It's because I'm 'nice,' isn't it?"

She looked at him strangely. "What are you talking about?"

"Tamika told me you like me because I'm nice," Ethan said.

"Well, that's part of it. But what's wrong with being a good guy? Besides, you've got it all wrong, Ethan. I like you because we really get along. It just feels…*right*," she said.

He smiled. Then he shook his head. "But why did you need the drugs? I mean, I was nervous, too. But I just sprayed on some extra deodorant."

Kat shrugged. "You do your thing, and I do mine. It's no big deal, Ethan. It's just pot. It's not like I do *real* drugs. I don't take pills, and I'd never be stupid enough to use needles. That stuff will just mess you up. I just wanted to relax." She looked at him. "Are you telling me you've *never* tried it?"

"Never," Ethan said.

"Are you serious?"

Ethan nodded.

Kat couldn't seem to believe it. "Wow!"

Ethan felt a bit embarrassed.

"I'm sorry," she said. "Huh. I just thought everyone had tried it at least once."

"I guess not," Ethan said.

Kat smiled. "I guess not."

"Does that bother you?" Ethan asked. "Does it make me seem too much of a good guy?"

"No. You're just right. Does it bother you that I smoke up sometimes?"

"I don't know. I guess not."

"Good. So, what else do you want to know about me?"

She's being totally honest with me. Cool. Ethan reached across the table and held her hand. "Can I buy you a coffee?" he asked.

Kat grinned with delight.

chapter 8

the mighty Zoltan

After school on Wednesday, Ethan sat on the green sofa in Kat's house. He was trying to write down all of Kat's game ideas as fast as he could. Her green eyes seemed electric.

"That's when Zoltan comes to take her away," Kat said.

"Wait a minute. *Zoltan?*" Ethan said. "Just *who* is Zoltan?"

"The dark prince," said Kat.

"Okay. So what is he doing there? I mean, when does he appear?"

"When Cassandra—"

"She's the hero, right?" Ethan cut in.

"Cassandra is the *heroine.* As I was saying, Zoltan appears when Cassandra passes through the tree of secrets."

"Where is the tree of secrets?" Ethan asked.

Kat sighed. "It's in the eternal forest. Man, Ethan. Weren't you listening?"

"Yes!" he insisted. "But you didn't say anything about a forest."

"Yes I did," she said.

"No, you didn't."

"I didn't?"

Ethan shook his head.

"Oh. Well, anyhow, Zoltan comes to take her away to his castle of evil—"

"Is that in the eternal forest, too?"

"Nooooo, it's on Mount Storm." Kat shook her head. "May I go on?"

Ethan nodded.

"Now the player has two choices. She can use her lasso of fire or her atomic crossbow."

"Wait a minute. Her *lasso of fire* or her *atomic crossbow*? That's not right. People from medieval times wouldn't have a lasso. They wouldn't have atomic stuff, either. It just won't work."

Kat sighed. "Stop worrying about the details. We've barely begun and you're getting stuck. Look at the big picture, Ethan."

"But no one will want to play it if it doesn't make sense! It will just be, well, stupid!"

"Grrrrrr. Big picture, Ethan!" Kat said.

Ethan backed off. "So now what?"

Kat shrugged and then took a deep breath. "Let's take a break. Okay?"

Ethan smiled. "Okay."

She went behind the bar and grabbed a couple of drinks. "Is root beer okay?"

"Yes, thanks." Ethan checked out her basement. He looked closely at the photos hanging on the wall by the pool table. Kat put on another CD and then came and looked with him. There were school photos of Kat throughout the years. In some she was freckle-faced and missing teeth. In others, she was the gorgeous girl standing near him. "Is this your family?" Ethan asked.

"More like our 'wall of shame'!" she said with a small giggle.

"Are these your parents?" He was pointing to a couple who looked like they were going to the prom. The guy had on a powder blue tuxedo. His hair was dark, curly, and huge! The girl had on a long, pale orange dress. Her long brown hair hung straight down her back. She looked just like Kat, except she had on bright green eye shadow.

"Yes," Kat said. "They met in high school."

"Oh. Where are they, anyhow? I haven't even met them yet. They're never here when I come by."

"They're working," she said.

"All the time?" he asked.

"Pretty much. They haven't been home before eight o'clock at night in months. My dad is on a business trip today. My mom is meeting a friend for dinner and a movie. Why do you want to know?"

"I don't know. I just thought they might worry about you hanging out alone with me."

"You really are cute, Ethan. Do you think I need a babysitter?"

"No! Of course not. I didn't mean it like that. I just meant that they've never even met me. For all they know, I could be some creep. I could be trying to take advantage of you or something. That is…they *do* know about me, don't they?"

"Sure," she said. "Well, they know I'm seeing someone. They just haven't asked me much about you. They like to think that the less they know, the better off they are. They're convinced I'm still a kid. If they don't ask questions, then they don't have to know the truth. So why should I tell them more than they want to know? Right? Besides, it just gives us a chance to spend some time together. Alone."

Ethan leaned in close and kissed her.

"Mmmmm," Kat said. "Hey, do you have to be home soon?"

"No. Not really. I told my mom I was working late on a project. It's a school night, after all," Ethan said, rolling his eyes. "Why?"

"Because I've got an idea."

He watched as Kat went into a back room and came out with another can of soda.

"But I just started this one…" he began.

Kat sat on the leather sofa and smiled. "It's not really a drink."

Ethan watched as she popped off the lid of the can. This was no ordinary can of soda. This one was a fake.

Kat dumped the contents onto the table in front of her. Ethan came closer to see what was inside. A pack of matches. A small booklet of white papers. Finally, out fell a clear plastic bag. It looked like it was filled with a pile of dried green leaves and seeds.

"What's that?" he asked.

"Pot," she said.

"Oh!" Ethan couldn't believe what he was seeing. Kat had a stash of drugs. "Are you really going to—"

He didn't need to finish the sentence. Ethan watched as she took a piece of the rolling paper. She filled it with a line of crumbled marijuana. Then Kat rolled the paper into a thin cigarette. She twisted the ends and held it under her nose to sniff it. "There," she said. Kat struck a match and lit the joint. She closed her eyes and inhaled deeply. Then she offered it to Ethan.

Ethan stared at the joint. A million thoughts went through his head. He thought of every stupid teen movie he'd seen. Every lecture from his parents rang in his ears. Every smart reason to say "no" hung over his head. *I know what I should do*, he thought. *I should just leave. Make some excuse to get out of here.* But somehow no words came out of his mouth.

Finally, he said, "I have a test tomorrow. I haven't even studied for it yet. And I was going to drop off some notes at Carlos' house."

Kat shrugged. "Study for it in the morning. Meet Carlos before school." She was still holding out the joint. "Are you going to take it?"

"I don't know," he said.

"Why not?" she asked. "You said you don't have to go just yet."

Think of something to say. "Uh, where did you get this stuff anyway? Is it yours?" He was trying to stall for time.

"Uh huh. It's from Ray."

"Ray? Oh," he said, trying to sound relaxed. *Great. Now I look like an idiot for not trying it. AND I look like a dork compared to her ex.* "Did you smoke up with him?"

"Sometimes," Kat said. She inhaled again and didn't speak for a minute. Finally she said, "It's burning up. Are you sure you don't want some?" Smoke curled out of Kat's mouth as she talked. "It's good stuff. I don't want to waste it." Kat paused again. "Hey, don't do it if you don't want to. It's no big deal. I just thought we could get more creative. You know, come up with some good ideas for the game. You trust me, don't you?"

Ethan's mind went blank. He couldn't think. Not when he was looking at gorgeous Kat Matthews. Kat with the deep green eyes that seemed to sparkle. Kat with the long, silky hair that brushed along the edge of her smooth cheeks. Kat with the soft red lips, which he could still taste. Kat.

Ethan knew he was supposed to say "no." But there was a secret part of him that was curious about what it would be like. He wasn't sure what to do.

Then Kat lightly touched his knee as she settled back into the sofa. A jolt rushed through Ethan's body. He gathered up his nerve. Then he reached for the joint.

chapter 9

don't try this at home

It took five minutes for Ethan to stop coughing.

"Ethan! Are you all right?" Kat asked.

"Sure," he wheezed. "It's smooth."

Kat only grinned at him. Then she closed her eyes. "Relax," she said. "Just listen to the music."

It seemed like twenty minutes went by before she spoke again. By that time, the CD had ended. She slowly got off the couch and went over to the stereo. Ethan followed her.

"So, how do you feel?" she asked him.

"I don't know. The same, I guess," he said.

Kat grinned. "Just wait. Besides, isn't this better than studying?"

Ethan nodded. He began to forget all about Carlos and the test. "Yeah. It's just one test. Hey, what are you going to put on next?" he asked.

"Whatever," she said as she looked through her CDs.

"Oh."

"Do you like 'Red Hot Rain'?" she asked, opening a CD case. "Their new stuff is smokin'."

Ethan grinned. "You mean, it's hot?"

She giggled. "Yeah. Wet hot."

Ethan tilted his head and thought about it. "Wha—?" Then he giggled, too.

Before they knew it, Kat and Ethan were doubled over in laughter. Tears ran out the corner of Kat's eyes. Ethan tried to speak. "That's so lame. Wet hot," he said, laughing.

"I know!" she said, holding her stomach. "It's stupid, but I can't stop!" Then she laughed so loudly that she actually snorted.

Ethan fell to his knees. "Stop!" he groaned. "It hurts. Too…much…laughing!"

Their laughter slowed down to a giggle. Finally they stopped. They sat in silence for a moment. Then Kat said, "What were we talking about?" She rolled onto the floor beside him.

Ethan shrugged. "What?"

They lay side by side, looking up at the ceiling and listening to Red Hot Rain. Somehow the music made Ethan feel happy. He felt inspired. He reached for his sketchbook and pencil and began to draw. Kat pulled herself up and watched him create characters for her game. She began to make suggestions about what he should create next.

"This is brilliant!" Ethan said.

"Yeah. We *rock!*" said Kat. Her eyes looked totally dazed.

"Rock and roll!" Ethan giggled. Suddenly he said, "I'm starving. We really worked up an appetite."

Kat laughed. "I don't think that drawing made you hungry." She crawled toward the bar and reached behind it for a bag of potato chips. Then she tossed it back to Ethan. It hit him on the head.

A moment later he said, "Hey!"

They tore open the chips and shoveled them into their mouths. They tasted great. Kat was about to get another bag when Ethan sat up straight. "What was that?" It was like a radar went off in his head.

"What was what?" Kat said.

"That noise. I heard a noise."

"I didn't hear anything."

Ethan jumped up and listened. "There's somebody here!"

"Take it easy, Ethan. We're alone."

Ethan sniffed his shirt. "Oh no! I reek like pot!" he cried.

"So what?" she said.

"It's the cops! I know it! They can smell me. They know we've been smoking up. They're going to arrest us." He looked around wildly. "I've got to get out of here." He grabbed his coat and pushed past Kat, who was on her feet now.

"Ethan. The cops aren't here," she said.

But Ethan didn't hear her. He flew up the stairs and burst out the back door. Kat stood in the doorway watching him. Ethan looked back once, then he ran home like a scared rabbit.

He hopped fences and ran through strangers' backyards. From time to time, he hid behind a tree to catch his breath. Ethan froze every time he saw the headlights of a car. He was convinced that the police had a drug team trailing him.

He finally reached his own backyard. Ethan hid in the shadow of the lilac bushes for half an hour. Then he tiptoed up the back stairs and opened the door. The door groaned. Ethan froze. He waited but no one came. Ethan continued through his house.

Where are they? he thought, looking for Paul and his mom. The sounds of the television floated down the hall. Ethan could see its lights flicker on the walls. *They're in the den*, he thought. *They must be watching a movie.*

61

All he had to do was pass the den door and tiptoe up to his room. Ethan bumped into the walls as he made his way to the stairs. "Shhhhh!" he hissed to himself. He crept up the stairs as quietly as he could. *Just get to your room. That's it. Slooowly. Be quiet.*

He reached his bedroom door and turned the handle. "Just about there," he said. He slipped into his room and blew a sigh of relief.

Just as he clicked his door shut, he heard his mother call, "Ethan? Is that you?"

Ethan froze. The hairs stood up on the back of his neck. Panic ran through his body.

Her footsteps were on the stairs. Ethan dove into bed, pretending to be asleep.

His mother opened the door. "Ethan? Why didn't you answer me?" She flipped on the light and started to speak. "Why are you in bed so early? It's only nine o'clock."

Act normal, he thought. *Be cool.* "Mom? Is that you?" he said sleepily.

"Ethan. What is going on here?"

"Oh. My…uh…head…uh…hurt. So I just went to bed." *Smooth*, he groaned to himself.

"Really? Do you want an aspirin?" She came over to his bed and felt his forehead. She cupped his chin and looked in his eyes. "Your eyes are red," she said.

"Are they? Oh. I must have a migraine," he said to her.

His mother was about to feel his head again, when she stopped all of a sudden. A strange look crossed her face. Then she leaned in and sniffed his hair and shirt. "What is that smell, Ethan? I need to know."

"What smell?" he said, trying to sound innocent.

"Your shirt. It smells like…" her voice trailed off. Then she shook her head. "It smells…strange. Where have you been?"

"Nowhere," he said.

Ethan's mother stood up. Her hands were firmly on her hips. "Ethan," she said, raising her voice. "What have you been doing?"

"Nothing!" Ethan said. "I was just out. That's all."

"Where? With whom? Answer me, Ethan!" She was almost yelling now.

"At a friend's house," he answered. "Kat."

"Kat? Who is Kat?" she demanded.

"My girlfriend."

"Oh," his mother said, softening a bit. "For a moment I thought you were doing…well, never mind what I thought. So you *do* have a girlfriend? Is she nice?"

Ethan nodded.

"Good." His mother paused. "But what is that *smell?*"

"Oh…incense. Kat lights incense. Because of the dog. It stinks," he said nervously.

"Oh." His mother didn't look convinced. But she didn't look like she was going to rip off his head anymore.

"Okay, then." She leaned down and brushed his hair. Then she tucked him in like she did when he was a kid. "Ethan…" she said.

"Yeah?"

"You would tell me if there was something going on. Wouldn't you?"

"Yeah. Sure, Mom," he said. *Please go away,* he prayed. *Please.* "I'm really tired, Mom."

"All right. Good night." She looked worried, but she turned out the light and left the room.

Ethan fell back on his pillow. He let out a huge sigh of relief followed by a little giggle. *Man. I can't believe she bought that.* Within a moment, he was sound asleep.

chapter 10

the morning after

Ethan strutted out of the classroom at school the next day. It was like he had a soundtrack to a movie in his head. In fact, the world seemed a lot different than it did the day before. Last night, he and Kat were brilliant. Ethan couldn't believe how creative they were together. *We make a great team*, he thought. He no longer felt like regular Ethan Munroe. He felt like he was on top of the world. A bit bad. And he liked it.

Halfway down the hall, he heard Damon Sanders call his name. For some reason, his good buddy didn't seem as much fun today. Ethan took a moment before he turned and waited for his friend to catch up. Then they both walked toward their row of lockers.

"How's it going?" Damon asked.

"Great," Ethan said.

"How was the geography test?" he asked.

Ethan stopped in his tracks. He hated to fail a test. "Not very well. Actually, I…uh…forgot to study for it."

"Really?" Damon said. "You were talking about it last week."

"Yeah," Ethan said. "I guess I was busy last night." *More like wasted.* He grinned to himself.

"Too bad," Damon said. He was about to say something else when Carlos came up behind them.

"Hey, man. What happened to you last night? I needed those notes from geography class. I wanted them to study for the test," Carlos said to Ethan.

Guilt flooded over Ethan. "Oh no! I forgot. Sorry, Carlos."

"Don't worry about it," Damon said to Carlos. "You've got an 'A' in that class already."

"True. But next time don't let me down, man," said Carlos. Ethan nodded and looked away. "But never mind about the test. Did you guys hear the news?"

"What news?" Damon asked.

"There's supposed to be a narc here at Bayview," said Carlos.

"A narc?" Ethan asked.

Carlos nodded. "Yeah. It's like a police officer who works in disguise. Like a teacher or a student. Someone who looks for drugs. Kind of like a spy."

"Get out!" Ethan said.

"I heard the cops could even bring in police dogs to sniff for drugs," Carlos said.

"Oh yeah. I heard they did the same thing at Port Hope High last year. Some guy was even charged for dealing," said Damon.

"Isn't that normal for 'Pot Hope'?" Ethan said. Then he took a look at his jacket hanging in his locker. The faint odor of marijuana filled his nose. Or was he just imagining it? *I wonder how long that stuff is supposed to stay in my body? What did we learn in health class? Was it over a week?* "Who told you there was a narc?" he said, feeling a bit nervous now.

"No one. I mean, I heard Tyson Richards telling that Riley Jackson guy in the hallway. So it's got to be true. Tyson's dad is on the police force," Carlos said.

Ethan shook his head. He was trying to make sense of what Carlos was saying. "I don't know. A narc? Nah. This sounds like something out of Tyson's head. Besides, we'd totally know if there was a narc here. Right? It would be too obvious." Ethan looked at his friends. "Hey, what if it's old Mr. Phipps, the librarian?" he joked. "Come on. How could they think we wouldn't notice? I don't believe it."

"Yeah," agreed Damon. "Why would they need a narc? The police would just have to come in and see for themselves. It's so obvious where to get drugs."

"No it's not," said Carlos.

"Sure. Drugs are everywhere," said Damon.

Ethan wasn't sure what Damon meant. "I didn't think there was any hard stuff here at Bayview. Are you talking about cocaine? Isn't that stuff way too dangerous? And isn't it supposed to cost a lot of money?" he said.

Damon gave him a weird look. "Who said anything about coke? I'm talking about dope."

"Come on. It's not like pot is a *real* drug," said Ethan.

Damon shook his head. "Sure it is."

"Well, it's not like anyone flips out on it or anything," Ethan said.

Damon shrugged. "I don't know about all that. But the stuff still is illegal. Why risk it?"

"And getting arrested can't be a good thing," Carlos added with a grin.

"I still don't see what's the big deal. Lots of people smoke up," Ethan said. But for some reason he didn't feel so sure of himself anymore.

chapter 11

is she with you?

The hallway was filled with the clanging of locker doors. Ethan put away his books. Carlos waited for him while Damon went over to his own locker. *Those guys don't know what they're talking about,* Ethan thought.

He looked up. Kat and Tamika were walking toward him. Kat was wearing her funky denim hat. Her hair was tied back in a ponytail. Just the sight of her changed his mood. For the better.

"How are you doing today?" Kat said as she arrived at his locker. She waved hello at Carlos. Carlos nodded back.

Ethan grinned. "Excellent," he said. He saw Tamika smiling at him. "Hi!"

"Hey, Ethan," she said in a friendly voice.

Kat continued. "So you're feeling good? Glad to hear it. We've all got to let loose now and again," she said with a wink. "So what are you doing now?"

Ethan noticed that Kat had on her jacket. Her car keys were in her hand. "I've got chemistry. Where are you going?" he said.

"The Edge. Do you want to come?"

"You're going for coffee *now*? Don't you have a class?"

Kat said, "Yeah, but it's just phys. ed. I don't feel like running laps today. Are you sure you don't want to come? You look like you could use an extra-strong coffee, babe." She gave him a private look.

"Are you going, too?" he asked Tamika.

She shook her head. "No, I've got English now. In fact, I'd better get going. See you guys around." Tamika waved good-bye and walked toward her next class.

"So are you in?" Kat asked again.

"No thanks," Ethan said. "I'll see you later."

Kat leaned over and gave him a quick kiss before she left. By this time, Damon had finished at his locker and had come to join them. His jaw hung open.

"What?" Ethan said. He smoothed his hair, looking in his locker mirror.

Damon continued to stare at him. "What do you mean, *'what'*?"

Ethan shrugged and smiled.

"What's going on? You're not seeing Kat Matthews, are you?" Damon said.

"Maybe I am…" Ethan said.

"Whoa! When? How? Why?"

Ethan glared at his friend. "We like each other. Is that so hard to believe?"

"Yes it is. But don't get me wrong. Kat is gorgeous. But you've got to admit that she doesn't seem like your type. Or maybe, *you* are not *her* type," Damon said and grinned. He jabbed Carlos in the ribs with his elbow.

"Not you, too?" Ethan said to Damon. "And why does everyone say that? Am I ugly or something? Do you think I'm a loser?"

"No, I don't mean that. I guess you look okay. Hey, what do I know—I'm a guy. But no one ever said you were a loser. Kat just doesn't seem to care about what anyone thinks. She seems to do what she wants to do. And she's kind of out there, sometimes, too. And you're—"

Ethan cut him off, "I'm *what*?"

Carlos pretended to look around. The mood was getting tense.

"You like to keep things safe," Damon said. "Besides, what do you guys have in common?"

"We have plenty in common! Like we're both creative. Besides, so what if she's laid back? I didn't know it was wrong to have a girlfriend who didn't act exactly like me."

"Girlfriend? Who has a girlfriend?" a soft voice said. Shelby came up from behind and wrapped her arms around Damon's waist. "Hi, babe," she whispered. He turned around and kissed her.

"I do," said Ethan proudly.

"Really?" said Shelby, with surprise. "That's great, Ethan. Who is it?"

"Kat Matthews," Ethan said.

Shelby and Damon exchanged a look. Then she turned to Ethan. "Kat Matthews? Are you sure she's right for you?" she said with concern.

"What's so wrong with Kat?" said Ethan. He was completely annoyed at his friends.

Damon sighed. "There's nothing wrong with her. It's just that you guys hang out with different people. Her friends seem—"

"They seem *what?* You met Tamika. She's great. Or is there something wrong with her, too?" said Ethan, his arms crossed.

Damon shook his head. "Let me start again. *Some* of her friends seem…well…wilder than you. Wasn't her ex and that other guy busted by the cops for drugs?"

Ethan couldn't believe what he was hearing. "So she has some wild friends. What has that got to do with *Kat?* Besides, you don't even know her."

"You're right. We don't know Kat," said Shelby. "But we do know some of her friends."

"That's right. *SOME* of her friends. You see? You don't know everything. What's wrong with you guys? Normally I would've thought you'd be happy for me. Friends are supposed to support each other, you know. But I can see that you've got a problem with that," Ethan said.

"We're just telling you to be careful. And what about Ray? I didn't think they were over. I don't want to see you get hurt," said Shelby.

Ethan's face grew dark. He looked at her. Then he glared at Damon. "Well, it's too late for that, isn't it?"

Damon looked away for a moment. Then he spoke quietly. "I thought we got over all that."

"*Whatever*," Ethan said through gritted teeth. "You know what? I think I just figured it out. You guys are jealous."

"*Jealous?!*" Damon and Shelby said together.

Carlos gave a nervous little laugh. "Uh oh," he said in a low voice. "Here we go."

chapter 12

show down

Shelby and Damon were stunned.

"Why would we be jealous?" Shelby asked.

"Yeah, man. Why would we be jealous of you? Shelby and I are together. I'm not interested in Kat," said Damon.

Ethan shook his head as if to clear it. "No! I meant that you guys are jealous because I've moved on."

Shelby and Damon still looked confused. Carlos rubbed the back of his neck. Ethan was fuming now.

Ethan looked to Shelby. "I don't know. Maybe you want to think I still have a thing for you. Then there's you, Damon," he turned back to his friend. "You must feel good knowing I wanted to be with your girlfriend. That she picked you over me." Ethan's face was turning red. "But now *I'm* with someone who is amazing. And you guys can't stand it. I've moved on, and you don't like it!"

By this time, a crowd had started to form nearby. The raised voices drew the other students in close.

"Do you really think that?" said Shelby.

Ethan shrugged. "Maybe it feels good to pity me. There goes poor Ethan. Boo hoo."

"You're nuts," Damon said. "Pity? Is that what you think? Do you really want to know what I think? You're not man enough to deal with us being together."

"Not man enough? Are you joking? Anyway, what kind of a low-life jerk takes his friend's girlfriend?" Ethan said.

"What?!!" Damon and Shelby said at once.

"You know it's true," Ethan said. His fists were gripped tightly.

"First of all, Shelby was *never* your girlfriend. Second, Shelby and I've liked each other for a long time. We just held off because we didn't want to hurt you."

"Ethan, what's really going on?" Shelby said. "You're not acting like yourself."

"I *am* being myself. You guys just can't handle who I really am. If you want to go out with a back-stabbing person like Damon, then be my guest. Maybe you two deserve each other after all."

"What are you talking about?" Damon said.

"You heard me," said Ethan, and he poked Damon in the chest.

"Hey!" Damon yelled. He threw down his books. They scattered over the hallway floor.

"Cut it out, guys. Mr. Thomas is watching," Carlos said.

Ethan looked up and saw the teacher standing two doors down. Mr. Thomas raised his hand to get their attention.

Carlos moved between his two best friends to hold them apart. Ethan just pushed Carlos out of the way. "Don't touch me," he growled.

"Calm down," said Carlos. "We don't pity you. Right?" he said, nodding at the other two.

Damon looked away. He was fuming.

Shelby shook her head. "No, Ethan. Think about it. Do you really think we pity you? We're your friends. Don't be silly. Of course we want you to be happy."

"And you're not much fun when you're unhappy," Carlos tried to joke.

Ethan glared at him. "Don't start," he said.

"It's a joke, Ethan," Carlos replied. "Relax."

"I *am* relaxed," he said through tight lips.

"*Riiiiight*," said Carlos.

"We just don't want you to go out with someone for the wrong reasons," said Shelby.

"Wrong reasons!" Ethan said. "What are you talking about? What are the right reasons?"

"I mean, don't do something just to prove a stupid point," said Shelby.

"What point? What am I trying to prove?" Ethan demanded.

Carlos spoke again. "I don't know. Maybe Shelby thinks you're trying to compete with Damon. That you can get a girlfriend, too."

"Is that what you think? Well, I'm not going out with Kat because I want to be cooler than Damon. I *am* cooler than Damon. And why are you on his side anyway? It's not like anyone is beating a path to *your* door. How many dates have you been on lately?" Ethan said to Carlos. He knew he'd touched a nerve with him now.

Carlos glared at him. "What has any of this got to do with me?"

Now Ethan taunted him. "Maybe *you* can't handle my relationship with Kat. Mr. Big Shot Basketball Star can't even get a girlfriend, but *I* can. HA!"

"Low blow, man. And totally out of line. You don't know what you're talking about," Carlos said. His voice was filled with anger now.

"I know I don't need this. In fact, I don't need you." Ethan slammed his locker shut. He pushed his way past Damon, knocking him in the shoulder.

"Fine by me," Damon growled.

Ethan stormed toward the main doors of the school. He slammed them open with all his might. Ethan pushed through the crowd of students on the steps.

"Hey!"

"Watch out!"

"Slow down, buddy."

Ethan only felt his anger. In fact, he didn't hear Kat shout his name. He was halfway across the school lawn before he heard her calling him. He turned and waited at one of the oak trees.

Kat greeted him with a happy smile. "Ethan! Where are you going? Didn't you hear me?"

"What? Oh. I was just thinking," he said with a scowl.

Kat frowned. "What's wrong? You're acting weird. Are you okay?"

Ethan sighed. "I'm not sure what I'm supposed to feel like anymore." He looked back at the school. "I think you might be the only one who understands me now."

"Do you want to talk about it?" Kat asked with concern.

"No. Not right now."

"Okay, no worries. Why don't you blow off the rest of school today? Come with me. If you don't want to go to The Edge, then we can go to my place. Tomorrow will be better," Kat said.

A slow grin crossed his face. "You're amazing," he said to Kat. "Maybe you're right. Let's get out of here. I couldn't sit through classes today, even if I wanted to." He put his arm around her waist and pulled her close.

"Oh yeah? Why is that?" Kat said in a low voice. She wrapped her arms around his neck.

"My mind is on other things today."

"Like what?" she said, nuzzling his neck.

"Oh, I don't know…" He leaned down and softly kissed her.

"Mmm," Kat said, grinning. "So, Mr. Munroe, what do you want to do now?"

Ethan felt like he was on top of the world. The anger he'd felt turned into something else now. He felt wild again. A rebel. And it felt good. "Get high," he said.

A sly look crossed Kat's face. She seemed to be amused by the change in Ethan. And a bit attracted, too. *"All right,"* she said.

chapter 13

4:20 p.m.

On their way to Kat's car, Kat and Ethan bumped into some people Ethan didn't know. They seemed to know Kat, though.

"Hey!" said a guy with short, blond hair.

"What's up?" said a girl with long, red curls.

A guy in a faded leather jacket just nodded.

"We're going back to my place to spark up," said Kat.

"Cool. We're in," said the first guy.

"Wha—?" said Ethan. He was stunned. *I thought this was going to be time with Kat. Alone.*

"Cool," said the other guy, ignoring Ethan.

"Great," said the girl.

"You don't mind, do you, Ethan? These guys are a blast. I promise you'll have the best time," Kat said.

"Well, uh, if you say so," he replied. A heavy feeling began to grow in the pit of his stomach.

"Great! Get in," she said to her friends.

"The more the merrier," Ethan said, forcing a smile. *Not,* he added in his head.

The redhead just rolled her eyes at Ethan.

Now Ethan was wedged between the blond guy and the girl. The other guy was called "Scud." He sat beside Kat and played with the stereo. *More like Crud,* Ethan thought. As if he heard Ethan's thoughts, Scud popped in a CD and cranked up the volume. The car started to vibrate with the music. Ethan could feel it pounding in his chest. Kat screeched out of the parking lot.

"Kat!" Ethan said, but she didn't turn around. She couldn't hear him over the music. "KAT!" he yelled.

"What?" Kat said, finally.

"Are your parents home?" Ethan shouted. Scud had just turned down the stereo. Ethan, however, was still yelling. They all laughed, except for Ethan. He just felt like an idiot.

Kat giggled. "Nope. They'll be back late. Maybe midnight."

"Oh," Ethan said. A few minutes ago, getting high seemed like a good idea. That was until he ended up with a group of total strangers. And one of them was named Scud. *What am I doing here?* Ethan said to himself.

In Kat's house, Scud went straight for her stereo. He started flipping through the albums. A few moments later, the sound of a screeching guitar cut through the room. The girl, Allie, made her way to the bar fridge. "Hey, Kat. Is there anything to drink?" she said.

"In the back room," Kat said. She turned to give Ethan a kiss. "Having a good time?"

"Sure, great," he said.

Allie came back with a couple of drinks. Vic, the blond guy, picked up a pool cue. He started to sink the pool balls into the pockets.

It was as if this was a normal gathering of friends. Ethan almost forgot why they were all there. Then it happened. The group started to take things out of their pockets and backpacks.

Vic set up some tubelike thing. It started to gurgle and smoke, and he breathed into it. Ethan watched, amazed. He could feel his jaw hang open. Vic looked up and stared back at Ethan. "Hey, buddy. What are you staring at? Take a picture, man. It might last longer."

"Sorry," Ethan muttered.

Allie pulled out her make-up bag. She searched in it until she pulled out a small foil-wrapped package. Inside was a brown chunk.

"Do you want some?" she said to Kat.

What's that stuff? Ethan wondered.

"No, thanks. I'm good," said Kat. She had already dumped out the contents of her soda can stash. Kat was rolling a joint. Then she lit it and inhaled. "Ahhhh," she said. She sat on the floor and leaned back against the sofa. Scud reached over and took the joint from her.

"Hey!" said Kat. "Now I have to roll another one." She started to make another joint. When she finished, she offered it to Ethan.

Ethan hesitated. He was trying hard not to look as though he didn't know what was happening. An hour ago, Ethan felt wild. Cool. Now, in this group of strangers, he didn't feel comfortable. Last night, smoking up with Kat seemed okay. She didn't laugh at him. He felt like a new person with her. But this was a different scene than the night before. He didn't know these people. He didn't know what they would do. In fact, he didn't know what some of them were *doing*.

"Come on, Ethan. It was your idea." She winked at him.

Ethan knew she was right. *I can't wimp out in front of these guys,* he thought. He sat down beside Kat, took the joint from her fingers, and inhaled deeply.

83

chapter 14

buzz

A wisp of smoke slowly rose up above Scud. It hovered over his head like some strange halo. Scud stared at Ethan for a long time. Then he spoke. "So, uh, Evan."

"Ethan," he replied.

"Right. That's what I said. So, Evan, what's up with you, man?" Scud continued.

"Excuse me?" said Ethan.

"You and our Kat…"

"Oh," Kat answered for him. "Ethan and I are working together. He's an artist…" Her voice trailed off. Ethan could feel himself smile.

"He does some wicked sketches," Kat said after a while.

"Really?" said Scud, who didn't seem interested at all.

"Feeling good yet?" Kat said, looking up at Ethan. Her head was resting in his lap now. She looked happy.

"Yeah. I guess so. I think," he replied.

"Loosen up, Ethan. Enjoy yourself. Hey, wasn't I right? Aren't these guys great?" she said happily.

"Sure," he said. Ethan looked around. He felt completely out of place with Kat's friends. For the first time, Ethan felt like he *was* out of Kat's league. Kat took the joint back from him and inhaled. Then she passed it back. He paused and then inhaled again.

Sometime later, Ethan was feeling a lot more relaxed. *Maybe Kat is right. Maybe these guys are great. I just don't know them. They don't know me. Maybe they've just got to get to know me*, he decided. "I like to draw!" he blurted out.

"What?" said Allie.

Vic started to laugh loudly. "I like to draw," he said, imitating Ethan. He almost slid out of the chair because he was laughing so much.

Normally, Ethan would have felt like a fool. But now he was high, and he didn't care.

"Hey, back off, guys. Ethan is really helping me," Kat said.

"He's helping *you*?" said Scud.

"Yeah. With that game," she said.

"Game? What game?" said Scud.

"The...uh...one with the...uh...castle! Yeah! Castle! That's it!" She giggled.

Scud broke into a smile. "Cool."

"Are you *still* working on that thing?" Allie said slowly.

"Yeah. So?"

"But you've been doing it *forever*. You'll never finish it."

"Sure I will. Ethan is helping," said Kat.

Ethan thought this would be a good time to speak up again. "Yeah. I like castles."

They all started to laugh at him. This time, Vic fell out of the beanbag chair and onto the floor. The group broke into even louder laughter. "Good for you, buddy," Vic said, pulling himself back into the soft, round chair. He couldn't seem to stop giggling.

Ethan was confused.

"You *guys!*" Kat squealed. "Ethan is awesome. He draws great..."

"Great what?" asked Scud.

"What? Oh...I don't know," she said, dazed.

"Castles?" added Scud.

They all laughed again.

Ethan tried to ignore them. "Hey, Kat. I have a great idea for another game," he said.

"Huh?" she said.

"Goblins," said Ethan proudly.

"What?" Allie said.

"Goblins. They're kind of like elves. They'd be great for a game," Ethan explained.

"Goblins?" said Vic.

"Yeah," said Ethan. He felt like this was the most brilliant idea he'd ever had. Kat *was* right. Pot made him creative. He felt like a genius. "Goblins. Bee-eating goblins. NO! *Purple* goblins. And they could wear yellow-striped hats, and they could…uh…sing! No. They could yodel when they're in danger!"

"Did you say 'purple, bee-eating goblins that yodel'?" asked Scud.

"Yeah," said Ethan. He sat back with a huge smile on his face.

"Cool," said Kat.

"Yeah, cool," said Allie. She looked dazed, too. "I think I can see them now." She sat back and stared at Bongo the dog.

"Hey, I'm hungry," said Scud suddenly.

"Me too! Who wants pizza?" said Vic.

"I do," said Allie.

Scud got up and searched for a phone book. He ordered some food and then went to check the music again. Half an hour later, the food arrived. Scud carried down two large pizza boxes. The hot food smelled delicious.

"Finally," Vic said.

Ethan waited for his turn for pizza. Scud said to him, "Hey, Evan. The pizza guy needs some money."

"So?" said Ethan.

"So pay him," Scud said, annoyed.

"Why me?"

"I'd do it, but I'm broke. Look, I'll pay you back later. I'll give the cash to Kat, okay? Okay. Great. Now move over. I'm hungry," said Scud.

Ethan looked around to see if anyone else was going to pay. The group didn't seem to see him. They were too busy eating pizza. In fact, no one paid any attention to the pizza guy at the door. He was calling for someone to come back and pay him. Ethan got up and went upstairs. He felt like he was moving in slow motion. He was beginning to feel *very* strange.

By the time Ethan returned, they were all munching on pizza. Vic was talking. "Speaking of exploding...I was sick as a dog last week. It was the worst stomach flu I've ever had."

Kat giggled. "The *flu?* Don't you mean *hangover?* I've seen how much beer you can drink," she said.

"Nah. It wasn't that. It must've been that nasty hamburger from Lee's Restaurant. Hey, someone should call the cops on that place," Vic said. "That burger should've been against the law, man."

Scud smiled. "Yeah. Call the *food* cops."

"The food cops?" Ethan said, startled. "Who are the food cops?" He started to panic. "Are there really food cops? Are they like the regular cops?" Soon he grew wild with fear.

Scud gave a wicked grin. He stretched out his leg and nudged Vic. "Sure. Everybody knows about the food cops. Right, Vic?"

"Huh? Oh yeah," said Vic. "Sure. The *food* cops. Got it." He winked at Scud. Then he turned to Ethan. "Yeah, man. And I hear that they're after *you!*"

"Me?" Ethan was shocked. "Is it the drugs?" he whispered quickly.

"Yeah, man. That and your—"

At that exact moment, a fire engine raced by. Its sirens were blaring. "That must be them now," Scud said, laughing.

"Really? I've got to get out of here," said Ethan. He bolted up the stairs and outside. The sound of laughter floated up behind him.

chapter 15

trust me

This time, Ethan didn't know where to go. So he didn't go anywhere. He hid in the evergreen bushes in front of Kat's house, trembling.

After a while, someone came outside. It was Kat. She was staring at the sunset.

Ethan remained as still as he could so as not to rustle the bushes. He didn't feel safe talking to her. After all, the food cops could be out there. Waiting for him. *Then again, they might get Kat, too,* he thought, worried. He watched as she stumbled past his hiding spot. In a flash, he reached out and grabbed her hand. He yanked her back into the shadows with him.

"Wha—?" she shrieked.

The next thing Ethan felt was the hard point of Kat's elbow in his stomach. He crumpled to the ground and moaned in pain. He felt like he was going to throw up.

Kat knelt down beside him. "Ethan? Is that you? Are you hurt?"

Ethan moaned some more.

"Well, good!" She giggled. "What did you think you were doing? I thought you were some jerk out to get me." She held out her hand and helped him up. "Why are you in the bushes? I thought you left."

"I'm hiding," he said, clutching his gut. "Sorry for grabbing you. But I thought the… uh…food cops were going to get you, too."

"The *food* cops? Seriously? Those guys were just yanking your chain. There are no food cops, babe." He gave her a look that said he wasn't totally convinced. "Trust me. I'm sure. You're being paranoid," she told him.

"Paranoid? Me? No, I'm not." Then he added quickly, "What do you mean by that?"

"You see! You *are* paranoid. You think everyone is out to get you when they're not," she said.

"How do you know they aren't out to get me?" he asked.

Kat stared at him and smiled. "It's the drugs. Some people get like that on pot. That must be what's happening to you."

"But you don't freak out," Ethan said, confused. His head was starting to clear. He was beginning to feel normal a little at a time. It took a while to think straight again.

"Maybe I'm used to it," she said and shrugged. "Who knows?"

"Yeah, maybe," he said quietly. "It feels kind of weird."

"What does?" she said.

"Being high."

"Oh. But do you like it?" Kat asked.

To be honest, Ethan wasn't sure. Kat didn't seem to have a problem with getting high. In fact, she really seemed to like it. As much as he wanted to fit in, Ethan just kept feeling like a total idiot.

Kat sat on the ground by the bushes. Ethan sank down beside her. He didn't know what to say. All he could think of was that stupid idea he had for a new video game. *Did I really say 'bee-eating goblins'? How stupid could I be?* He could still hear the sound of laughter in his head.

"Does it get better?" said Ethan, finally.

"Does *what* get better?" said Kat.

"The drugs," he said quietly.

She shrugged. "It's not the same for everyone. Some people feel more paranoid than you did. Some people never stop coughing."

"Maybe I just have to keep trying it. Get used to it," he said. But a tiny feeling in his gut made him doubt that idea. "I think I sound like a fool when I'm stoned. Those guys must think I'm such a loser." He nodded his head in the direction of her house.

"If it helps, Scud thinks *everyone* is a loser." She giggled softly.

That's because Scud is *a loser,* Ethan thought with a smile. "Well, are they always so *friendly?*" he said.

"They do what they want. They're okay. Besides, they're my friends."

"Oh. They seem more like buddies, to me," said Ethan.

"Buddies. Friends. Same thing," said Kat.

"I don't think so." Ethan thought about it. "I mean, say you had a problem at three o'clock in the morning. Would you call those guys to help you?"

"I don't know. Sometimes Scud can get me some pot when I'm out. Is that what you mean?" Kat said.

Ethan shook his head. "No. I'm not talking about that. I mean, if you had an emergency. Like, say you had to go to the hospital and you needed a ride. Would you call Scud? Would he come over?"

"I guess not. But who would be happy helping *anyone* at three in the morning?"

"I would be," said Ethan. He looked over at Kat. Her eyes were closed. She was so pretty. She just didn't seem to care about anything. Nothing seemed to bother her. *I think maybe she really likes me, too. I hope.* Then Ethan grew determined. He was going to make his relationship with Kat work. He was going to prove it to everyone. He thought of Kat's friends again and their reaction to her game plans. He wanted to prove it to them, too. "Kat, what did those guys mean about your game?"

"What do you mean?"

"Well, how long have you been working on it?" he asked.

She shrugged her shoulders. "Maybe a couple of years. I don't know. It takes a while to get inspired. You know…to come up with a good idea and then make it work." She turned to Ethan. "That's what's so great about you. You help me stay focused."

"I do?" he said with a smile. "Good. So, who is this guy Ray knows at that video company? When can we meet him and show him our stuff? I've been thinking about the battle scene for the game."

"Cool," said Kat.

"Maybe we could work on it again soon."

"Maybe." Kat took his hand and rested her head on his shoulder.

They stared at the evening sky. The sun had turned the clouds shades of orange and red. The blue sky was slowly growing darker.

Ethan still felt a bit confused about it all. At first, Kat really wanted to put together a game with him. Now she just didn't seem to care. "Hey, Kat? Were you *really* serious about your game? Like a 'get it done' kind of serious?"

"I think so."

"Then we should do it for sure. We should show everyone that we can do it. That we're a great team."

"Okay," she said. "Whatever you say. But now I think I'm going to have a little sleep…"

chapter 16

high noon

The next couple of weeks were a blur. Ethan spent most of his free time with Kat. A lot of the time they were high. Most of it he didn't remember at all.

One Friday morning, a loud banging woke Ethan out of his sleep. "Ethan! Are you up yet?" his mother yelled. "You're going to be late for school. Again!"

"Who cares?" Ethan shouted back.

"I care!" said his mother. "And so should you. Why are you still in bed?"

Ethan groaned. "It's just math. I already know how to count."

"Unless you're sick, get up! If you don't get up, I'm calling the doctor!"

"I'll get up."

"When?" she yelled through the closed door.

"When I feel like it!" he called back.

BANG! BANG! BANG! His mother went on pounding. "You can't sleep the day away. You have school. And I have to go to work. I'm going to be late."

"So GO!" said Ethan. He pulled his feather pillow over his head. He could hear her sigh loudly. Her nagging faded down the hallway and out the front door. A minute later, his mother revved the engine of her car and then drove off down the street.

"Peace at last," Ethan said and then fell soundly asleep. Later, he opened his eyes and tried to read his alarm clock. "Eleven o'clock. I guess it's time to get up," he said sleepily. "Maybe I can make it to school for lunch." He pulled himself out of bed.

Slowly, Ethan made his way downstairs. He stumbled into the kitchen. He noticed a note and a twenty-dollar bill stuck on the fridge door. The note was from his mother.

Ethan, please pay for the newspaper tonight. You forgot to do it last week. And please leave the paper-girl a tip this time. Paul and I won't be home for supper. We're going to a couples' workshop. Love, Mom.

Ethan opened the fridge, searching for some breakfast. "I'm starving," he thought aloud.

"Is that right?" said a voice behind him.

Ethan whirled around. "What the—?"

"Good morning, Ethan. It's good to see you up so early," Paul said with a sly smile.

Ethan caught his breath. "What gives you the right to sneak up on people like that?"

"Are you a bit on edge today?" asked Paul.

"No!" said Ethan quickly.

"We need to talk," Paul said.

Ethan looked at him suspiciously. *What is he getting at?* he wondered. "I'm not in the mood to talk," he told Paul.

"You haven't been yourself lately."

Ethan opened a cupboard and pretended to look for more food.

Paul continued. "I'm talking about the drugs. You've been getting high. It's time to talk about it."

Ethan's heart began to pound wildly. *Oh, man!* He tried to avoid Paul's eyes. *What am I going to say? What is he going to say? Is he going to freak out on me? No. He's not yelling. Not like Mom. Or Dad, if he knew.* "I don't know what you mean. I'm not doing drugs," he lied.

"I am not going to argue with you," said Paul. His voice was steady and even.

Man! thought Ethan. *Okay. Don't say anything else. Stay calm.* Ethan remained quiet. He could feel Paul's eyes burning into his neck.

Ethan couldn't take it anymore. "Look, Paul, *you* are not my dad. You can save the lecture for someone else."

"So is that it? Does all of this have to do with your family situation? Look, I know this family can be...well...difficult. You have two sets of parents. One of which you hardly see. You have a new brother. Life is not what you thought it was going to be. Or wanted it to be."

Ethan snorted. *This is the stupidest speech I've ever heard.*

"I'm not going to ask you why you've been doing drugs. You have your reasons. I just want you to think about what you are doing. Really think about it. Ask yourself *why* you are getting high. Ask yourself if it's the answer to your problems. How is your life different since you started doing it? Is it easier now? And for what? A high that lasts a few hours? Deep down you know it isn't worth it. I care about you, Ethan. And whether you choose to believe it or not, I am on your side. We all are. We're here to listen," Paul said.

Ethan rolled his eyes. "Gee, thanks, Paul. But you *weren't* listening to me. AGAIN! I said

I wasn't doing anything. It figures you wouldn't believe me."

"I know what you said," Paul replied calmly. He wasn't letting up.

"Are you calling me a liar?" said Ethan.

"I'm just pointing out the facts. And the fact is, you smell like pot." Paul looked him in the eyes. "Your friends have changed. You've been skipping classes. You sleep a lot more now. And look in the mirror. Your eyes are bloodshot again. And you can't seem to do simple things like pay the paper-girl. Your actions have changed. So has your attitude."

"Nothing is different," Ethan said.

Paul continued, "It's your choice, Ethan. And I hope you choose to quit. You can *always* talk to your mom and me. Your dad and Sue care, too."

Ethan laughed. The thought of his mom crying and getting angry didn't seem appealing. Nor did the thought of his dad yelling and flipping out. "You're way off."

"Ethan, we all have problems."

Ethan just stared at his stepfather. "This is unbelievable. This is like a scene from one of the worst movies I've ever seen. Are you done?"

Paul looked carefully at Ethan. "Yes," he said. "For now."

chapter 17

they just don't get it

The clock in the chemistry room seemed to stop moving. He couldn't concentrate on the lesson. In fact, Ethan didn't seem to care at all. All he could think about was going to see Kat. And getting high again.

Carlos was also in class today. He tried to get Ethan's attention, but Ethan ignored him. He pretended to be reading his notes instead. Carlos leaned over to talk to him, but Ethan tuned him out.

"Hey, man. Are you all right?" asked Carlos, nudging Ethan's arm.

"Fine, thanks," said Ethan.

"Are you talking to us yet?"

"What do you think?" answered Ethan.

"I think you're still crazy."

"Get lost," Ethan snapped. He didn't really know why he was so mad at Carlos. He just needed to be mad at *someone*.

"Fine. Be that way. You know where to find me when you cool off," said Carlos. He turned around and faced the front of the room.

Ethan stared at the clock. The second hand ticked closer to twelve. At the sound of the bell, Ethan bolted for the door. He was the first one out of the classroom.

The hallway was filled with the sounds of Bayview students ending their school day.

Ethan could see Damon and Shelby. They were leaning against Damon's locker. As usual, they were all over each other.

Shelby looked up and waved at him.

Ethan gave a small nod. Then he looked at Damon, and they exchanged a hard stare. Finally they both nodded, but they never said a word.

"I can't believe you guys are still being idiots. Make up and move on," said Shelby.

"There's nothing to talk about," said Damon.

"I'm still waiting for you to say you're sorry," said Ethan.

"Sorry for *what?*" said Damon.

"You know *what*," Ethan replied.

"No, I don't. You're the one who should say it to me," said Damon. "You're nuts, man."

"I must be," said Ethan, and he grabbed his jacket. He turned and slammed his locker so hard that his mirror fell off on the inside. When he turned back, he saw that Shelby was pointing at him.

"What?" Ethan said.

"Your sketchbook," said Shelby. "Are you making some sort of art statement now?"

Ethan looked at the cover of the book he was holding. He had drawn a large marijuana leaf on it. "Oh." He smiled. "Do you like it?"

Shelby shook her head in disgust.

Kat approached, slowing down as she neared Ethan's locker. Ethan carelessly pushed past Damon when he saw Kat come near. "Hey, beautiful!" Ethan said to her.

"Hey there, yourself."

He gave her a deep kiss right in front of Damon and Shelby. After a long moment, he pulled back and wrapped his arm around her.

"What was *that* for?" Kat giggled.

"I'm just happy to see you," said Ethan. "Are you ready to go?"

"Sure! Let's rock," she said.

With his arm around Kat's waist, Ethan led her through the hallway. He paused and looked over his shoulder at Damon and Shelby. "See you later, *buddy*," Ethan called.

Kat looked up at Ethan. "What's wrong?"

Ethan frowned. "Those guys still don't understand us." Out in the sunshine, Ethan turned to Kat. "But it's great to see you." He leaned down and kissed her again.

"You're sweet," she said. They reached Kat's car and got inside. "So, what do you want to do now? Do you want to hang out at The Edge?"

"Nope. I thought we could work on the world's greatest video game today."

"What?" said Kat. She seemed confused.

"Your game! Remember? We were going to finish it so you could show it to your contact. Then it would be nothing but fame and fortune," Ethan explained.

She shook her head. "I'm not in the mood today. Too tired."

"Me too. But I thought this game was really important to you. I even remembered to bring my sketchbook."

Kat still didn't look sure. "I don't know."

"We make a great team, Kat. We can do this!" said Ethan proudly.

Kat paused. "If you really want to. Okay. Let's do it," she said and pulled out of the parking lot.

"Game on!" Ethan said, laughing.

"Riiight!" she replied.

chapter 18

return of the
dark prince

Back at Kat's house, Ethan looked through his sketchbook. Kat pulled out her laptop computer.

"So, where did we leave off?" she said.

He showed her what they'd created earlier. "We were making obstacles for the players," he said. "And here are some sketches I made when we were high." He looked at the pictures and scratched his head. "What is this?"

"Show me," said Kat. She took his sketchbook and began to giggle. "Oh yeah! I remember. We decided to make a bright pink tree frog. And it would wrap its mile-long tongue around people and squeeze them."

"Aren't tree frogs really tiny?" said Ethan.

"I think so. But this frog was going to surprise its victims by break dancing. The players get startled, lose their balance, and then fall off the drawbridge."

"I don't believe it. Did we really come up with that?" he said.

"Yup. It must've been the drugs," she said.

"But, we were so creative."

"Think again! Well, at least it's funny."

"More like stupid," said Ethan. He took back his sketchbook and flipped through some more pages. "Is that it? I thought there was more than this."

Kat looked at the book. "I guess not."

"Weird," said Ethan. "Oh well. We'll just work harder today. So, what do you want to happen at the second level? Should we make a deformed crocodile?"

Kat opened her laptop and began to type up some ideas. A half hour passed and Ethan sighed. He noticed that Kat was just staring at her computer screen.

"What's the matter?" he asked her.

"I'm stuck," she said.

"In the chair?" he joked.

Kat rolled her eyes. "No. I need something exciting to take place. But I can't come up with anything else."

"Let's take a break. Maybe we could use some *inspiration*," he said with a slow smile.

"Inspiration? Do you want to get high again? You really are a bad influence on me, Mr. Munroe," she teased.

"Yeah. It might help us loosen up. You know, get some good ideas going."

"Like the bee-eating goblins or the pink frogs?" she said with a wink.

"You bet." He didn't feel like working right now, anyhow. "So, are we on?"

"Okay. But I'll have to make a call first."

"Why?" he asked.

"We used up the last of my stash last time. I have to get some more."

"Oh. Right," he agreed.

"Do you have any money?" she asked.

"Not much."

Kat stared at him. "Can you get some? I'm broke. You'll have to pay this time."

"Maybe I've got some at home. Let me see if I can dig up some extra cash."

"Great. We'll stop by there on our way to The Edge," she said.

The Edge? Why are we going there? Ethan wondered.

Then Kat picked up the phone and dialed. "Hello, Ray? I need to meet you. I need to score some more weed."

chapter 19

dial·a·dope

Kat pulled into the driveway of Ethan's house, and he ran to the back door. Inside, he quickly looked for any sight of Paul or his mom. The coast was clear.

Ethan hurried through the house and raced up the stairs to his room. He desperately searched through the pile of junk on his dresser. Video magazines. A copy of *The Bayview Post*. The model car he made when he was twelve. CDs. Socks. "Come on. Where is that money? I'm sure I had some extra cash," he said to himself as he overturned the piles. "Nope. Nothing. Hmmm. Maybe it fell on the floor." He crouched on his hands and knees and looked under his dresser. Nothing. "Man! I know I saw it somewhere. But where was it?"

Ethan searched his memory. Then, like a lightning bolt, he remembered where he'd seen the cash. "That's it!" he said. "The money to pay for the newspaper."

He tore downstairs. It was still stuck to the fridge door. A crisp twenty-dollar bill. Ethan reached for the money. *It's not your money*, he heard a voice say in his head. *You're stealing*. A twinge of guilt ran through him. He shook his head. *I'll pay it back*, he thought. *I think I have some CDs I can sell.* Then he pocketed the cash.

Ethan locked the door behind him and then jumped into Kat's car.

"Did you get it?" she asked.

"Yeah, let's go. Tell me the plan again?"

"We're going to The Edge," explained Kat. "Ray is playing there tonight."

"And he'll have the pot for us?"

"That's right. He's meeting his contact first. Then Ray will give us some of his."

"You mean, *sell* it to us," corrected Ethan.

"Of course," she answered.

"So does that make Ray your *dealer*?"

"Ethan! You make it sound like I'm some sort of addict. No! Ray is not my *dealer*. He just knows somebody who can get me some more stuff. That's all. He's just passing something to me from a guy he knows."

"But we *are* paying him for it," Ethan continued.

"Well, of course."

"What if the cops show up?"

Kat laughed. "Ethan, it's not *really* a drug deal. Okay? We're just paying Ray for some weed. And *no*, the cops won't show up."

"Are you sure? Wasn't Ray busted for drugs before?" he asked.

"Yes. But that was totally unfair. The cops were *so* wrong to pick up Ray. They should've gone after the *real* dealer. Not Ray. At least they haven't bothered him since."

"What about the narc?" he asked.

"What narc?" She sounded annoyed.

"The undercover cop who's supposed to be working at Bayview."

"I don't know what you're talking about. In fact, I'm not sure what's going on in your head. This was your idea, Ethan. If you don't want to get high tonight, then don't. But I went through all these plans just for you. Ray is waiting. What do you want to do?"

Ethan thought for a moment. "You're right. I guess I've just got that rumor of the narc in my head. I'm cool with going to The Edge tonight."

"It's a good thing because we're here," said Kat. She pulled into the parking lot.

"I'm going in," Kat said and got out of the car. Ethan got out, too. "Maybe you should wait here," she said to him.

"Don't you want me to come with you? You know, for protection?"

Kat laughed. "It's okay. Besides, Ray doesn't know you're with me."

"I thought everything was cool between you guys. That you were just friends."

Kat sighed. "Yes, but it's hard to explain."

"Well, explain it to me just one more time, Kat. I've noticed that you can be pretty protective of Ray."

She stared at Ethan. "Don't get the wrong idea. Look, Ray and I have a history together. It's hard to get past it sometimes. But for the last time, you have *nothing* to worry about."

"I don't?" he said, as a slow smile crept across his face.

She leaned toward him and kissed him. "No. You don't."

Ethan pulled back gently and looked in her eyes. "Okay," he said. "Then let's go." He grabbed her hand and pulled her toward the coffeehouse.

Inside, the music had just stopped playing. The place was busy. Tamika was working tonight. So was Troy. And there, by the front window, were Carlos, Shelby, and Damon. Shelby tried to get Ethan's attention. But Ethan still ignored his friends. He wasn't ready to talk to them. Not until they took back what they said about Kat.

"There he is," Kat said. She nodded at Ray, who was taking a break.

Ray looked their way and came over. "Hey," he said to her.

"Hey," said Kat.

Ray and Ethan sized each other up. Ray turned back to Kat. "I don't have your stuff yet," he said.

"Really? Why not?"

"My guy is running late. He should be on his way here now. I'll give him another call," Ray answered.

Kat looked at Ethan. Then she looked at Ray. "Maybe it would be better if we waited outside for you."

Ethan noticed that Troy had moved through the crowd, too. He was carrying a tray of small cups. He would stop and talk to customers at each table. He started to talk to the curly-haired guy behind them. "Would you care for a free sample of our latest drink? It's whipped toffee supremo," he said. The customer shook his head. Ethan watched as Troy continued nearby.

Ray took his cell phone from his back pocket and dialed. "Hey, man. It's me…"

"Let's wait outside," said Kat. She led Ethan outside. They stood in silence under the black awning of The Edge.

"Look, Kat. I'm sorry about what I said about you and Ray. I just really like you."

Kat nodded. "I know."

The air was warm, and a soft breeze was blowing. It was a good night to be out. The place was busy, as usual. Customers strolled in and out of the coffeehouse. People were crowded on the patio. Cars filled the parking lot.

Out of the corner of his eye, Ethan saw a dark car enter the parking lot. It circled the lot slowly. Then it parked in a far corner. No one got out. A second car entered and did the same thing. It parked closer to The Edge.

The hairs stood up on the back of Ethan's neck. "Look at those cars." He pointed to the dark cars with the darkened windows. They couldn't see who was inside. "I don't have a good feeling about this," said Ethan.

chapter 20

big, black boots

Kat shook her head. "Maybe they've just come for some coffee."

A few minutes later, a shiny, low, red car entered the parking lot. It parked nearby. Then another dark car entered the lot. This one sat near the entrance.

"This is interesting," said Ethan. He watched the driver of the red car talking to someone on his cell phone. A few minutes later, Ray came out of The Edge. He looked around and then went over to the red car.

Now Kat was interested in the scene. They watched Ray lean into the driver's side window of the car. He seemed to be handing the guy something. Then Ray stuck something inside the front of his pants. Next, the guy gave Ray what looked like a small plastic bag. Ray held it in his hand. Then he nodded to the guy and walked away.

Ray calmly strolled over to Kat and Ethan. He looked as though he had done this a hundred times. Ray nodded to Kat and Ethan. Then he held out his hand to shake Ethan's, like they were best buddies. "How's it goin', man?"

Ethan was confused but shook his hand anyhow. "Fine," he said.

"Did you get the stuff?" Kat whispered.

The guy in the shiny car started to drive away. Ethan watched as he pulled out toward the main road. A police car with lights flashing sped in front, blocking his path. Then the dark car near the entrance blocked off the parking lot. Three people got out of the other dark cars and were moving quickly toward Ethan, Ray, and Kat.

Ray and Kat had their backs to the lot, but Ethan could see it all happening. They stopped talking when they saw Ethan's eyes grow wide. Ray looked over his shoulder and swore loudly.

"RUN!" Ray yelled.

Then instinct took over, and they ran. Fast. Ethan caught a glimpse of Kat running in the other direction. With Ray. Ethan was too terrified to think. He bolted through the parking lot, dodging between cars. He glanced back over his shoulder. The largest man he'd ever seen was chasing him! Ethan panicked.

"Stop! Police!" the man shouted.

Panting, Ethan ran as fast as he could. He had no idea where he was going. The cop's big, black boots pounded on the pavement behind him. The sound sent a chill through Ethan's body. He was coming closer. Ethan looked around quickly for an escape route. It was too late. A strong hand grabbed the back of his shirt.

The cop knocked him to the ground. Ethan felt the force of a knee against his back, holding him down firmly. The cop pulled Ethan's arms behind his back and pressed his face into the pavement. Gravel and cement rubbed hard against his cheek and nose. It was all so swift and hard. And painful. A set of cold, hard handcuffs clasped tightly around his wrists. "AUGH!" Ethan cried.

Once the officer was sure Ethan couldn't move, he removed his knee from Ethan's back. Next he checked Ethan's pockets and patted down his legs and chest. It took a moment, but Ethan realized he was searching him for weapons and drugs.

"I don't have anything," Ethan said.

The officer didn't say a thing. He just continued his search. Finally, he pulled Ethan off the ground and led him across the parking lot. Ethan was in shock. His body trembled.

By this time, two more marked police cruisers had arrived. The flashing lights lit up the window of The Edge. Ethan saw Kat and Ray. They were in handcuffs, too. Ethan watched as a female officer spoke to Ray. It sounded like she was reading him his rights. Then she put Kat inside the car, too.

"What's happening?" Ethan said to the officer who was holding him.

"Your friend is being charged," the cop replied. "We're taking him to the station. He'll be spending the night in a very cozy cell."

Ethan's eyes grew wide. "What about her?" he asked, nodding toward Kat.

The cop didn't answer. He was busy handing Ethan over to one of the cops who'd just arrived.

Ethan shook his head. "I told you I didn't do anything. I don't have any drugs. I didn't buy any. You can't charge me!"

The first officer kept calm. "Is that right? It didn't look that way to us, buddy. At any rate, you were in the wrong place at the wrong time."

The new officer put his hand on Ethan's head. He firmly put him into the back of the cruiser. He slammed the door and sat up front with his partner. They were going downtown.

chapter 21

the end?

Nothing could prepare Ethan for the ride in the police car. The stench was horrible. The mixture of stale vomit and old urine made him gag. It didn't help that it was boiling hot inside, either. Sweat started to bead on his forehead. He looked over at the windows. They were closed. Then Ethan saw a clear divider between the front and back seats. It was covered with spit, blood, and something Ethan didn't want to recognize. "Gross," he said.

He leaned back against the seat and tried to get comfortable. It was useless. The more he leaned back, the more the handcuffs tightened and cut into his skin. His hands were beginning to feel numb. He eventually sat near the edge of his seat. Ethan swayed and jerked with the car as it made its way to the police station. His head even banged into the divider a few times.

Once there, the police took Ethan into a small interview room. One of them took off his handcuffs and allowed him to sit in a chair. All of a sudden, the cop was being nice. He placed a tape recorder on the table in front of Ethan.

Ethan didn't know what to do. "I don't want to talk to you without my lawyer here," he said.

The officers grinned. "You've watched too many crime movies," one of them said.

"Well, don't I get a phone call or something?" Ethan continued.

"You'll have a chance to talk to a parent or guardian later. First we have some questions for you," one of the cops told him.

"But I *told* you I didn't do anything wrong. Not *really*," Ethan said to them.

"Well, that's not what your girlfriend said," one of the officers told Ethan.

Ethan's eyes flew open. "What? What did Kat say?" he asked. His head felt light.

The officers looked at each other. Then one of them spoke directly to Ethan. This time he sounded very serious. "She said it was all *your* idea. That *you* set up the deal with Ray and his contact. That you were jealous of Ray, and *you* tipped us off."

"You're wrong!" he said. "Kat wouldn't lie like that. I know what you're trying to do. You're trying to set me up!"

The first officer stared at Ethan. "I suggest you tell us what happened tonight."

Ethan looked at the cops. They were large, strong, and they meant business. Ethan had no idea how he got to this place. All he wanted to do was have some fun. Get high. Now he was sitting in a police station. Being questioned by people with guns. He gulped and looked down at his red wrists. He rubbed the spots where the handcuffs had broken the skin. Ethan took a deep breath and slowly raised his head. "Okay," he said. "Here's what happened…"

The officers started to ask him questions. Who he was. How he knew Kat and Ray. What had happened. Ethan told them everything he knew. He figured he had no real choice. He didn't know what Kat had really said. There was no way he could match stories with her. In fact, he couldn't be sure they'd even questioned her yet. So he just told the truth. When he finished, Ethan let out a huge sigh. "So you see, I didn't *really* do that much."

"Well, I'm afraid you're still a part of all this," one of the officers said. "You were a witness to a serious crime tonight."

"Okay, I know what we did was wrong," Ethan admitted. "But, Ray *only* bought a bit of pot. Maybe enough for a few joints. Is that really the worst thing ever? Shouldn't you guys be doing stakeouts for more serious guys? You know, for the *big fish.*"

"Ray *is* a big fish. And he didn't just buy a 'bit of pot.' He bought enough drugs tonight to sell to a *lot* of people. He's in serious trouble. And now you could be called as a witness in court," the officer said.

Ethan froze with fear. He didn't want to stand up in court and say anything about anybody. He just wanted this whole night to go away. "You can't be serious. I'm not going to have to testify, am I? What makes you think I'd do that?"

"Ray tried to set you up tonight, too. You know that handshake he gave you outside The Edge? He was trying to make it look like he passed off the drugs to you. Just in case someone was watching. He was right. *We* were watching. We've been watching him for a long time. You picked the wrong night to buy some drugs from him. We can make you take the stand, Ethan. We can make you go to court. But think of it as a good thing. You're helping keep Ray off the street. You're helping make sure that no one else can buy crack or cocaine from him again. Ever."

Ethan was speechless. "C-c-crack? Cocaine?" he stuttered. "Ray just bought some marijuana. That's all. What are you talking about? And how did you know he was going to buy that much tonight?" Then an idea popped into his head. "Was there a narc at The Edge?"

"No. We've been watching Ray for a long time. We knew he was going to make a big move soon. Ray is not a small time guy, Ethan. He's a major player around here. But we have him now. With thanks to some quick officers and some concerned citizens."

Fear, confusion, and shock filled Ethan. He couldn't believe all of this was even happening.

"Okay, then. It's time to go." The police led Ethan out of the room. They took him to a waiting area behind the front counter. One of them pointed to a bench. Kat was already sitting there. "Sit there and wait," the officer said.

Kat turned and looked at Ethan. "Hey," she said. "Some night, huh?"

"Kat, what's going on? Is it true?" he said.

She didn't seem to be listening to him. "This sucks," she said.

"Did you really tell the cops that you had nothing to do with it? That it was all my fault?"

Kat shrugged. "Ray wouldn't have got caught, and we wouldn't be sitting here if it weren't for you. *You* wanted to smoke up tonight," she said.

"Are you serious?" Ethan said.

Kat ignored him. "Can you believe what they're doing to Ray? It's so unfair. They're treating him like some sort of criminal. You know, this isn't the first time the cops have been out to get him. Now, they're trying to make it sound like he's some major player in the drug world. I won't help them frame him."

Kat didn't seem to get it. She was completely focused on Ray. In fact, she didn't seem to care about Ethan at all. She seemed to have no problem with lying about what really had happened.

"You are unbelievable!" Ethan said to her. "I thought you really liked me! How could you do this? How could you lie about me? Kat, we're in serious trouble here. We were part of a DRUG DEAL. We were ARRESTED. I don't know about you, but this doesn't happen to me every day. In fact, it *never* happens to me. Now we could be called to testify in court! You know…take the stand, swear an oath, help send someone *you know* to jail. And do you realize how lucky we are? We could've been charged for having drugs, too. How am I going to explain this to my parents? This is HUGE!"

"Look, I'm freaked out, too," Kat said. "But it's not like you got into any *real* trouble. You're still not old enough yet. You'd get off with a less serious charge than Ray. He turned eighteen two months ago. It's going to be a lot worse for him." Then she stopped and looked past him. "Uh oh. My parents are here. They're really going to freak on me. My dad looks like he's been yelling a lot already."

Ethan looked up and saw Mr. and Mrs. Matthews walking toward the front desk. Mr. Matthews' face was beet red. The officer motioned for Kat to come over. She slowly got up. "Well, I'd better get this over with. The good news is that my parents will let it die down in a few days. They always do. They yell a lot. Threaten to punish me. But they never really do anything. I can't wait 'til it blows over."

Ethan gave her a hard stare. "So that's it? You sold me out to save *Ray*, and that's all you have to say? What about *you* and *me*?"

Kat looked down. "I'm sorry, Ethan," she said. "But I think Ray needs me more now." Then she walked away and didn't look back.

Ethan watched her leave. Thoughts began to swirl in his head. He couldn't believe that Kat had used him like that. He couldn't believe his friends were right about her. Ethan sighed. He knew it had taken a lot of guts for them to speak up before. Then he thought of how he'd talked to Carlos. He remembered the way he'd treated Damon and Shelby. Deep down he knew those two belonged together. Ethan felt horrible. He knew it was going to take a lot to make it up to his friends.

A police officer came up to Ethan. "I'm going to call one of your parents or guardians now. However, I see four names listed on your sheet. Who should we contact? We need to tell someone where you are and what's happened."

Ethan put his head in his hands and tried to think. No matter who the police called, it wasn't going to be easy. Finally he looked up. His face looked grim. "Maybe I could talk first? Would that be okay?" he asked the officer.

The police officer stared hard at him. "All right. But I'll need to speak to the person, too."

Ethan nodded and went over to the front desk. He picked up the telephone and dialed. Then he took a deep breath. "Hello, Paul? Yeah, it's me. I'm in trouble. I need your help."

glossary

advisor
A person who counsels or gives advice

cocaine
An illegal drug, also known as "coke," that looks like white powder. It is made from the leaves of the coca plant and is inhaled, or "snorted." Side effects are extreme and can be deadly.

crack
A form of cocaine that looks like white chunks or chips and is smoked

heroine
A female lead character

jasmine
A type of sweet-smelling flower

marijuana
An illegal drug, also known as "dope," "pot," "weed," "grass," and other nicknames. It comes from the hemp plant. The dried leaves and tops of the plant are usually smoked in cigarettes called "joints." Marijuana affects the brain and its ability to learn. Some people who use it can become addicts.

midway
The area of a fair or carnival that has rides

migraine
A severe headache

narc
A person who acts as a spy to discover
drug deals and use. The name comes from
"narcotics," or illegal drugs.

paranoid
Describing a person who acts with a strong
feeling of fear or distrust

pumping iron
A slang term for lifting weights

stakeout
To observe people without their knowing

storyboard
A series of pictures that show how the scenes
and plot of a story will take place

testify
To make a serious claim about a person or an
event. It is often made while under oath.

Special Thanks

I wish to extend my most sincere thanks to those people who generously gave their time, assistance, and support in the making of this book. For their expertise and help in authenticating the story, I deeply thank Alex Crews, Larry Dee, Natalie Stickles, Dominic Del Grosso, and Carol Del Grosso. For their careful reading of the text for interest, accuracy, and credibility, great thanks to Peter Hough, Nichole Sotzek, Maria Martella, Angela Dobler, Penny Knight, Lynn Lees, Jenn Lees, and Shani Bleich.

My most heartfelt thanks to my family, both immediate and extended, who helped me find the time and space in order to work and create.

Thank you to Ben Kooter and Vanwell Publishing for the opportunity and trust.

Finally, and as always, a great big steaming mug of appreciation and love to Tea Leaf Press.